# DIRTY GINGER

## THREE CHICKS BREWERY #3

## STACEY KENNEDY

*For everyone who has ever overcome a broken heart.*

Stacey Kennedy

www.staceykennedy.com

Edited by Lexi Smail

Copy Edited by Rose Perry

Cover Design by Regina Wamba

Manufactured in Canada

# DIRTY GINGER

The violinist played soft, classical music that drowned out the guests' soft laughter as Amelia Carter's six-year-old nephew, Mason, ran down the makeshift aisle. They were in the old barn that had been converted into Three Chicks Brewery, a craft brewery she owned with her two sisters. Amelia's insides felt like they were quivering. She'd never had an out-of-body experience before, but she was certain she was experiencing it now. Watching and listening to everything and everyone around her, yet feeling like she wasn't actually present, almost like she was a floating identity observing what should have been the happiest day of her life.

Clara, the eldest Carter sister, and Mason's mother, sighed, causing Amelia to turn toward her. Clara's deep blue eyes narrowed on her rambunctious son, his light brown hair bouncing atop his head. "Well, he got down there and the rings are still on the pillow. I guess that's a win?" Her gorgeous reddish-brown hair was set in big waves that flowed down her shoulders, reaching the top of the A-line lavender bridesmaid's dress.

Standing next to her, the youngest Carter sister, Maisie, laughed. "I thought that was going to go far worse, to be honest." Her blond hair was pulled up in a soft updo that highlighted the sweetness of Maisie's personality, and her dark blue eyes were still laughing when she strode by and walked down the aisle between the white chairs.

A cold wave washed over Amelia, stealing all the warmth out of her bones. The long veil covering her face felt like a much-needed curtain from the friends and family that soon would be looking her way. She woke this morning to a quivering stomach and the sensation stayed all day long. Something wasn't right. She kept telling herself she was fine, even though her high heel kept tapping on the gravel and her fingers kept fiddling with the lace of her mermaid-style wedding dress. But the very thought of walking down the aisle to her awaiting fiancé, Luka, nearly had her retching her breakfast all over the shiny wood floors.

Once Maisie reached the first pew, Clara turned around to Amelia. "Ready?" she asked gently.

Amelia considered the pointed question and searched for what was causing this feeling, wondering if perhaps it was due to her parents not being there. She and her sisters had lost their parents in a car wreck, and her grandparents stepped in to raise them. Maybe it was because her grandparents weren't there? The questions continued, but nothing felt quite right. Unsure how to answer, she nodded.

At whatever emotion crossed Amelia's face, Clara's typically hard expression softened. She grabbed Amelia's hands, squeezing tight. "You've got this. Trust me, the ceremony is the hardest part. After that, we party. Okay?"

Clara would understand her feelings maybe more than anyone else here. She recently got married to professional baseball player, Sullivan Keene, her high school sweetheart and Mason's father. God, what was wrong with her? Amelia let out a slow breath, telling those worried thoughts to quit it. She gave a firm nod. "Okay. Yes, I'm ready."

"Yes, you sure are," Clara said with a smile. "I'll see you down there." She hesitated, rare emotion filling her eyes. "You look absolutely beautiful, Amelia."

All the coldness broke apart under Clara's warm affection. She'd always been closer to Clara than to Maisie, even though in the past year, they'd all really bonded. But Clara had been a single mother for a long time. She had a tough skin most days, but Amelia saw none of that now. "Thank you, Clara. I love you."

"I love you too." Clara threw her arms around Amelia, giving her a long, tight hug that brought all the warmth back into Amelia's bones before she faced the guests again. With a deep breath, she headed down the aisle, leaving Amelia alone.

She told her feet to move. They refused.

Time seemed to slow down, her skin flushing too hot. Her mind began racing through the reasons she was hesitating, then quickly disposing of them. But she'd made this decision, and she loved Luka. They'd met her first year in college and they'd been together ever since. She wanted the marriage and the happily-ever-after. Amounting this to stage fright, she stuffed the remainder of those quivers away and straightened her shoulders, ready to get on with her future.

Off to the side of the groomsmen, the violinist switched to a different song right as Clara reached Maisie. Both her sisters smiled at her from the end of the aisle. Amelia hung onto that, the knowledge that this day would have made so many people happy. Especially her late parents and grandparents. And all the people here loved her. Deeply.

She started down the aisle, gazing over the guests as they rose from their seats; family and friends from all walks of Amelia's life, but her focus narrowed on one. Beckett Stone. His sandy brown hair never really had a style, and his gray eyes always screamed: *pure trouble.* He had been the man Amelia thought she'd marry one day. Her high school sweetheart. Also, her greatest disappointment. Beckett stood next to Maisie's fiancé, Hayes Taylor, with Clara's husband, Sullivan Keene, on his other side. Amelia had questioned inviting Beckett, but in the end, she wanted him there. Sure, they had a history, but within that history there had been a lot of love and a long friendship. For a split second, their gazes held, the world fading away to only her heartbeat thumping in her ears. All the unsaid things. All the lingering heartbreak from when she realized that Beckett wasn't the *one.* All the pain when he'd admitted they'd drifted apart and he had no interest in following her into the big city while she went to college.

She ripped her gaze off him, setting it on Luka waiting for her at the end of the aisle. Beckett broke promises. Luka hadn't broken a single one. But as she looked at her future husband waiting for her, she found his skin pale. A few inches taller than her, Luka fit into city life with his fancy suits, including the tux he wore now, and his styled dark hair.

When she sidled up to him, she smiled beneath her veil. He didn't smile back. He bounced from foot to foot.

The officiant began, "Today, we're here to celebrate—"

"Wait."

Amelia's blood ran ice cold at the desperation in Luka's voice. She'd never heard that voice come from him before. He mumbled incoherent things before he said, "I can't... I'm sorry, Amelia. I can't do this."

Gasps filled the space, loud chatter brushing across Amelia's ears.

A flush of adrenaline tingled through her body as she flipped up her veil. "What?" she snapped.

Luka looked over his shoulder at his parents and his

grandmother, who gazed on in horror. "I'm sorry," he said softly, his voice shaking. "I got wrapped up in it all. I—" He turned to Amelia. "I'm sorry. I can't go through with this. I don't love you anymore."

The world began to crash around Amelia as Luka nearly fell and spun to run away, only something stopped him.

Beckett's fist.

The punch hit Luka dead center in the nose. He soared backward, landing hard on the floor between the chairs, like all of Amelia's hopes and dreams.

The barn chilled with the heavy stillness until Maisie's sigh broke the shocked silence. "Now *this,* this I expected," she said.

*Two weeks later...*

At a little after nine o'clock in the morning, Amelia stepped out of the Uber, feeling like a different woman than the one whose life abruptly took a rattling sharp left into the trash fourteen days ago. "Thanks," she said to the driver, who had already gotten her luggage out of the trunk.

"Take care," the driver replied before getting back in his car and driving away.

Amelia faced the big, white, colonial-style farmhouse located in the small town of River Rock, in the gorgeous Colorado countryside, before she began climbing the porch steps. The house always held so much life. First, when her grandmother and her pops took her, along with her two sisters, in to raise them after their parents died in a car crash. Then when she lived in the house with Clara, Maisie, and Mason after their grandparents passed away. But now, as she opened the front door, she only met silence. Gone were her grandparents. Gone was Maisie. She had moved in with Hayes. Gone was Clara and Mason, living with Sullivan. Within the heavy silence lived the reminder that Luka had planned to move in here with Amelia. Now it was only her.

Refusing to allow the embarrassment and unbearable sadness to fill her again, she slammed the door shut on those thoughts. Literally. When she'd boarded the flight for their honeymoon to Saint Lucia the morning after Luka broke off their wedding, she'd done so with the intention of running away. Only, the lush forests, sunny skies, and the delicious rum for a whole two weeks had pulled her out of her despair and forced her to recognize a couple truths. She couldn't run any longer, and she had to face the fact that Luka hadn't been totally wrong – even she had doubts about their marriage. So she allowed herself three days of hiding in the hotel room dying of embarrassment and grieving the loss of the life she thought she was going to have with Luka before she spent the rest of her trip figuring out her new normal, thinking about what went wrong. But when she'd landed late last night and fell into the Denver airport hotel's bed, she decided that, now that she was back home, she'd have an open heart and an open mind, no more bitterness or shame.

Determined to pick up the pieces of her life, she set her suitcase down by the big wooden staircase, where a gallery of framed photographs displaying happy family moments hung. She took her cell phone from her purse and then headed back outside, approaching the brewery. She only reached the barn's double doors when she heard gravel crunching against tires. A quick look back revealed a big black truck with ROCKY MOUNTAIN BEER DISTRIBUTION written on the door.

The truck stopped, and Ronnie Keene exited with an unusually soft smile. He was a couple inches taller than Amelia and had light green eyes that always looked hard, serious in a way that unnerved Amelia most days. She wasn't a businesswoman like Clara, who usually dealt with Ronnie. He wore a Red Sox baseball cap overtop his bald head, supporting his nephew, Sullivan, who played for the team. But that smile as he approached, that soft, pitying smile, was all for Amelia.

"Good morning, Ronnie," she said, chipper. "Thanks for coming to meet me." She'd sent him the text on the drive back from Denver this morning, wanting to keep busy today. Especially since he'd sent her an email asking for a meeting with her as soon as she felt ready to have one.

"Mornin'," he said, shoving his hands in his pockets when he reached her. "Are you sure you're up to this meeting? Like I said in my text, we can wait—"

"I'm up for it," she said, giving him a bright smile in the hope of easing his worries. "I've spent two weeks relaxing, being spoiled rotten, and having fun. I feel refreshed and rejuvenated and totally ready to get back to work."

Ronnie gave her a nod and looked upon her with some-thing akin to pride. "Clara was saying you went on a trip."

Amelia nodded. "To Saint Lucia." What she thought would be two weeks to sulk had turned into fourteen days of healing. She'd even had some fun. "The trip was exactly what I needed, so please, truly, let's get back to work."

Another nod. "All right, then." He waved out toward the brewery. "Let's get back to work."

Good. One person had accepted her healed heart. Now she needed to get the rest of the nosy, overbearing town to get onboard too. She unlocked the barn doors, whisking them open, and her heart broke a little bit more. She'd had four batches of beer fermenting that she should have checked before leaving for the airport. She had intended to give instructions to her sisters to care for the beer while she was gone, but that had been the last thing on her mind. She could smell the rancid grain the second she walked through the doors. The state of her brewery was terrible, and that fell on Amelia's shoulders. "Ronnie, I apologize for this. Clara and Maisie don't know this part of the business, and I just left—"

"Don't," Ronnie said firmly behind her. "You don't need to apologize." He stepped in next to her and gave a reassuring smile. "I've got no doubt you'll get things up and running again and will meet all your quotas."

"Thanks for understanding," she said, leading him through the brewery into the back storage room to show him all wasn't a total bust. "We will definitely hit the quotas for this month."

Ronnie stepped into the room, scanned the already bottled cases of Foxy Diva, their top selling beer that Ronnie and his distribution company had recently picked up to distribute into every bar, restaurant, and store in North America. A huge feat for a small brewery owned by three sisters. "You always have this much stock on hand?" he asked, looking back at her with wide eyes.

She nodded. "I always make sure I'm ahead of the game." She didn't know what it said about her that she always planned for the worst. A result of losing her parents in a car crash and having her heart broken twice. She knew to stay ahead when things were good, because things always got bad again.

"This is good, Amelia," Ronnie said, turning in a circle. "Very good work." He returned to her, and she shut the storage room's door behind him.

"It won't take me long to get the brewery back in shape," she said, trying to breathe shallowly as to not inhale the sour aroma.

"I've got no doubt that's true," Ronnie said, walking next to her down the aisle between the tanks. He stopped at the barn's double doors again, visibly breathing a little deeper now too, crossing his arms. "The reason I sent you the email for the meeting is we had a marketing meeting while you were gone. Foxy Diva is doing well. Really well. But we'd like to draw more interest for the brewery next year. The team suggested we put out a special beer each quarter."

Amelia's mouth went dry. "Wow. That's an amazing offer."

Ronnie nodded. "It's something we've seen work very well with another brewery we've got. The only hitch is we've only got one spot for this type of distribution and three breweries in our roster competing for the spot." He paused, pressing his lips together before continuing, "I realize the pressure this would put on you. If you're not ready, or up for it—"

"I'm up for it," Amelia sputtered before even considering it. Maisie had made their little brewery successful in the beginning by traveling to beer festivals and getting their name out there. Clara was the very reason Ronnie picked up Foxy Diva and distributed it. Now Amelia needed to prove her worth.

Ronnie laughed softly and gave a small nod. "I figured you would be ready." He glanced back into the brewery, tapping a cowboy boot against the ground. "Take a couple months. Brew six different ale samples. After that, we'll run some tastings and see what four come out as the leading contenders."

"Totally doable." Amelia smiled, her pulse racing over the idea of creating some new beers. She hadn't stretched her mind this way since she took Pops' home brew recipe and adjusted the ingredients, turning the beer into Foxy Diva. Yet at the same time, the little voice in her head worried that she couldn't take on such a huge undertaking. Six beer samples on a sound mind was hard, and her mind felt... shaky. "Thank you for your trust is our product, Ronnie."

"No thanks required," he said. That pride was back in his eyes. "You're a talented brew master, Amelia. You've got a good thing here. Don't forget that, without your talent, the brewery would not be where it is today."

Leaving her speechless at his kind words, he strode away. Ronnie rarely offered praise, and she knew it came from trying to boost her confidence after it had been so publicly depleted. Appreciating his kindness regardless of his reasons, she waved as he drove away. Then with the heaviest sigh of her life, she faced the tanks. Never in her life had she ever left her brewery in this condition. Her teacher, Graham Neal, would drop dead if he set foot in her brewery. "*Sanitize. Sanitize. Sanitize.*" had been his motto. Dust was in places it shouldn't exist. A tank was left open, obviously one of her sisters wanted to clean it and then changed their minds. Likely Maisie.

"You're home."

Startled at the smooth, low voice behind her, Amelia whirled around and found the last person she thought she'd see today. Beckett stood between the double doors, looking as hard as ever. Not only his muscular frame either, but his eyes. Not that she blamed him. Beckett's childhood was no walk in the park, and he wore those scars. "What are you doing here?" Her voice came out snappier than she intended, and she quickly softened her voice, "Sorry, I mean, I wasn't expecting you."

He didn't seem affected and lifted a lazy shoulder. "I've been keeping an eye on your place and saw a truck in the driveway. Came to check it out, but then saw it was Ronnie." He entered the barn, then scrunched his face and backed out. "Did something die in here?"

She nodded with misery. "Yeah, beer did."

"Now that's a damn shame," he said with a familiar half-smile. One she'd seen through all their years together. One she once thought she'd see every day for the rest of her life.

"Yeah, it is a shame," she agreed, leaving the barn doors open, hoping to let the space air out a bit before cleaning began.

"How was Saint Lucia?" he asked, stepping into stride with her, heading back toward his massive dark grey Ford F-150 parked near the house.

"Stunning," she answered. "The nature trails were out of this world. Beautiful hiking. Gorgeous weather. The place is so lush and alive."

"From what I saw, it looked it."

She slid her gaze to him, studying his expression. He avoided her gaze. It occurred to her she shouldn't have been so surprised he'd looked into where she went. Beckett was always the protector, including punching Luka when he'd wronged her.

Their breakup hadn't been because there wasn't love between them. Beckett was three years older, and before Amelia left for college, it became clear the direction of their lives had changed. While she'd cried many tears when Beckett ended the relationship, once she got to Denver for college, a whole new world opened up. Six months after she and Beckett ended things, she'd met Luka, and throughout her time at school, they eventually fell in love. When she finally returned to River Rock, the love for Beckett remained, only it was a different kind of love. Not so needy and desperate, but more familiar and comfortable – a very good friendship. No matter what, Beckett was there for her. Always. And she was there for him too when she could, though he was terrible at asking for help.

When they reached his truck, she faced him again. "Thanks for keeping an eye on the place while I was gone. I really appreciate it." She paused, realizing she had something else to thank him for. "And thanks for punching Luka in the face. I had definitely wanted to do that, but didn't have the mind to actually make it happen."

"You never have to thank me for that. I'll happily knock him out on your behalf anytime you'd like." His mouth twitched as he tucked his thumbs into the pockets of his jeans. "And as for your house, it's on the way to the farm, which I really need to get to."

Warmth carried through her, and she smiled as he headed for his truck and got into the driver's seat. Beckett had once been on his way to becoming a professional calf roper, but instead he now worked for Nash Blackshaw, who owned a horse training facility that rehabilitated troubled or young horses. The facility was a well-known staple in Colorado now. People came from all over the country to buy horses from the once famous bull rider, Nash Blackshaw. Beckett was a part of that, and Amelia always liked the special connection he had to horses and was happy he found his place in the world.

Once inside his truck, he rolled down the window and gave her face a long look with his strong gaze. "The trip looks good on you."

"Thanks," she said. "The trip felt good on me, too."

His soft smile made her smile too. "Good to have you home, Am." Only Beckett called her that nickname, reminding her of easier times when life was a whole lot simpler. He flashed her his charming grin that had once been all she could think about before he drove away, a trail of dust following his truck.

She waited until the truck vanished up the road before she let the daunting reality hit her. She had very little time to come up with one new sample, let alone six. Some of the darker ales had to ferment for five weeks, meaning she needed to get on her plan pronto. Sure, she'd been playing with a handful of new brews over the last year, but when Ronnie's company picked up Foxy Diva and put the beer into circulation, Amelia's focus had been getting ahead of supply and demand. But first she needed to deal with the messy state of her brewery. The rest she'd figure out later. Pushing the rising tension— that had all but evaporated in the tropics — away, she entered the house and shut the door behind her. The silence. It was everywhere and it was heavy, a reminder that her sisters' lives had moved on, and hers…

She shook her head, not allowing her thoughts to take her to that dark place. This was her new normal, and she had to move on.

Moving into the kitchen, she smiled at the tulips in the vase on the old, work oak kitchen table. The table held so many memories. Some good. Some bad. All family meetings, hard or otherwise, happened at the kitchen table. The spot had always been a safe place. A quick look in the fridge revealed it had all been cleaned out sometime since she'd been gone. That hadn't been Beckett. This was her sisters' touch. And as unsteady as things were, her family wasn't an issue. They were her rock.

A knock on the door came seconds before it opened, and her younger cousin, Penelope, called, "Amelia?"

"I'm in here," Amelia replied.

Penelope had moved to River Rock two Christmases ago and never left. Amelia was happy for it. Penelope handled the brewery tours that came in every weekend and knocked them out of the park. She'd learned the ins and outs of the brewery in record time, and she could now explain the beer making process without pause and answered every question flawlessly. Most of all, she was incredible with the public. People loved Penelope. Amelia could see why, she loved Penelope too.

When Penelope entered the kitchen, she looked as

gorgeous as ever. Her long brown hair was perfectly in place and her green eyes were sparkling with happiness. Amelia was glad to see it too. Penelope's horrible parents had shipped her off to live with Amelia and her sisters every summer at their grandparents so they could *enjoy* their summers traveling without her. Nevertheless, Penelope had created a good life in River Rock, and she deserved every little bit of happiness that came her way.

"Oh, girl, your tan is to die for," Penelope said, opening her arms wide.

Amelia walked straight into them, holding her cousin tight. "It's easy to get tanned when all you do is drink your face off by the pool bar."

"Nice," Darryl, Penelope's husband, said, entering the kitchen carrying two brown paper grocery bags. Scruffy-bearded, with dark brown-hair, Darryl was a cop with the local police department, and his amber eyes, while kind, held authority too.

Amelia studied the grocery bags, pressing her hand to her chest. "You brought me groceries?"

He set the groceries down on the kitchen counter. "Clara asked if we could pick you up necessities. She and Sullivan had a meeting with the principal this morning." Darryl threw Amelia a smile over his shoulder. "Mason got into a fight."

"Uh oh," Amelia muttered, only imagining how Clara reacted to that news. Likely not well.

Penelope laughed softly. "I've never seen Sullivan look so proud. Mason was just standing up to a bully."

Darryl began pulling the groceries out of the paper bags and setting them on the counter. "Sullivan's convinced he'll be a ball player, but I'm betting my money on him becoming a cop one day." At Penelope's nod of agreement, he turned his attention to Amelia, giving his serious look. "And you? How are ya?"

"Good." When they both just stared at her, she laughed to break the silence. "Honestly, I'm in a good place. I spent three days crying in my hotel room, hiding under the bedsheets, and ordering room service. But the trip was exactly what I needed, and I'm glad everything is over. I don't have to see or hear about Luka again, and life can carry on." Or at least that's what she would keep telling herself until she believed it.

Darryl cringed.

Penelope looked at everything but Amelia.

"What am I missing?" Amelia demanded.

Penelope and Darryl exchanged a long look before Darryl asked, "You haven't heard about Beckett?"

Amelia frowned at them. "I heard that he was watching the place for me while I was gone, but that's it."

"You haven't seen him?" Darryl asked.

Amelia looked from Penelope to Darryl, and her frown deepened. "He was just here, but didn't say anything. What's going on?"

Darryl set the basket of strawberries down, then turned to face Amelia, giving her his serious cop look. "Luka pressed charges against Beckett."

Amelia blinked. Processed. Heat tingled in her face. "You are kidding me, right?"

Darryl slowly shook his head, clenching his jaw. "I'm afraid I'm not, and Luka's not dropping the charges either. I've spoken to him on two occasions to follow up to see if he had changed his mind. He hasn't."

Amelia could barely believe what she was hearing, a tremor rocking her to her core. She gripped the counter tight. "Wait. Luka is really charging Beckett for a punch to the nose? Which he rightly deserved?"

Penelope gave a quick nod, taking out the bananas from the grocery bag. "I guess Beckett broke it real good. Luka's

17

health insurance covered the original break, but there's a bump on his nose now. Luka needs plastic surgery to correct it since it's not covered."

Amelia couldn't wrap her head around this, wanting to help put away the groceries, but feeling rooted to the spot. "What is Beckett facing here?"

"Luka is suing him for the money to cover the surgery. But Beckett will also face third degree assault, which is a Class 1 Misdemeanor," Darryl explained. "It could get him two years in jail and fines up to five thousand dollars."

A sick feeling sank into her stomach as the realization dawned on her. "This isn't the first time Beckett's had that charge." It happened after his twenty-first birthday. The judge had considered Beckett's clean history and he had ended up with probation and mandatory counselling.

"I know, that's the problem," Darryl said solemnly.

Penelope said, "Last time, they let him off easy because he was a first-time offender with a clean record. This time, it's not going to happen again, because to a judge, it looks like he has a history of violence."

Amelia pondered all this, and it all boiled down to one conclusion. "I need to go talk to Luka."

Darryl gave a grave nod. Though he didn't seem happy about it, he said, "Looks like it might be the only way to get him to change his mind."

Amelia drew in a long breath, processing everything that had happened since she got out of her Uber this morning. "Let me get this straight. I need to get the brewery cleaned, come up with six new beers as per Ronnie's request this morning, and mend things with my ex-fiancé that dumped me at the altar in order to save my ex-boyfriend from jail time."

Penelope smirked. "Welcome home."

## 2

Fifteen minutes after leaving Amelia, Beckett slowed his truck when he reached the wrought iron signage that read BLACKSHAW TRAINING, and he slid his tan-colored Stetson onto his head, feeling like he could finally breathe again. Amelia looked good. He never again wanted to see the haunted look in her eyes when he watched her heart shatter when Luka crushed her. He knew she had a long road of recovery ahead of her, but at least today she looked a little more like herself again. The gravel crunched beneath his tires as he drove up the driveway he'd driven up for the last two years, five days a week, sometimes more if a horse in training needed daily work. Horses were where his heart lay. He'd never questioned his decision to work at the training facility, and he never looked back.

He drove up the gravel driveway, passing by the two-story log house with the wide covered deck where Nash lived with his wife, Megan, and his son and daughter. The farm took in everything from young horses to trouble horses for training, and the facility had garnered a name for itself. People all over North America shipped their horses in for the care and training of Nash and the cowboys working for him. Beckett felt pride over the work they did, and that they saved many horses that otherwise would have been sent for slaughter.

When he stopped his truck next to the black-roofed barn, he spotted Nash approaching from the house. It took Beckett a minute to realize he had a carrier strapped to him with his daughter tucked inside. The view was such a contrast to the tough, rugged image of the famous, retired professional bull rider that it took a moment to process. But when he did, Beckett felt nothing but envy. Children, a quiet life, a wife by his side, he wanted all that and more. Which was why Luka breaking off the wedding was the best day of Beckett's life. It meant he could fix the biggest wrong he'd ever made. He could get Amelia back in his arms. When they dated, he'd been a reckless idiot who took his life day-by-day, living on the edge whenever he could. A wild mess of a man. When Amelia had spoken about going to college and chasing her brewery dreams, Beckett didn't want to stand in the way of her happiness. Knowing she'd never leave him to attend college, and with his father in River Rock, he gave Amelia a push to go, declaring there was a distance between them. At the time, he'd been stupid enough to believe she'd return home to him once she finished school. Instead, she met an asshole.

"I've got a new one in for you," Nash said by way of greeting as Beckett exited his truck. Nash skipped his usual cowboy hat this morning, and his messy brown hair and tired blue eyes indicated a few sleepless nights.

Beckett looked to the reason—Nash's daughter, Callie. She had the brightest blue eyes Beckett had ever seen, unusually aware, even though she was only five months old. He offered his finger and she squeezed it, bouncing her little legs in the carrier. "She looks far more awake than you do."

Nash laughed dryly. "Because we live in Callie's world now. She sleeps whenever she chooses, and we simply have to go with it."

Beckett chuckled. "Ah, tough like her mother, then." Nash's wife, Megan, was witty, sharp, and everything Nash needed to keep him in line.

"She is that," Nash replied, with obvious tender affection.

Callie released Beckett's finger and began eating her hand, and Beckett shoved his hands into his pocket. "About this horse."

Nash gestured ahead of them to the closest paddock next to the barn. Laid out in eight rectangular fields were grassy paddocks for the horses to graze. Behind the barn was a large meadow where the broodmares lived out their lives, raising their foals, which were later trained and sold. "The strawberry roan there."

Beckett took one look in the field and saw the fire in the horse's eyes. "Mare?" he guessed.

"You bet," Nash said. "She's got the attitude to prove it too."

Not all mares were made of fire and spice, but certain ones had that flavor. Beckett loved those mares the most. Callie began babbling as Beckett asked, "What do I need to know about her?"

Nash planted a boot on the lower railing of the fence. "She's got impeccable ground manners, but get on her back and you won't stay there for long."

A challenge. Beckett's favorite. "How dirty is she?"

"As dirty as it gets." Nash studied the mare before frowning at Beckett. "I worked her a little in the round pen when she got here. She's a bit of a puzzle. Confident in some ways, insecure in others. Seems agreeable with tack. Until you get on her."

Odd, but when a horse lost trust in humans, they could

act unpredictably. Beckett had seen this time and time again. He slid his gaze back to Nash. "How dangerous is she?"

Nash shrugged. "I haven't seen her act aggressively on the ground yet. But from what I hear, once someone backs her, she's determined to put a stop to that in any way she can, including flipping over backwards."

Which meant she'd learned the best and fastest way to get a person off her back. "Good to know." Beckett studied the horse, who watched him carefully. Horses were flight animals, and the mare was sizing him up as a threat, no doubt about it. "Has Dr. Alan had a look yet?" Dr. Alan owned River Rock's Veterinary Clinic for large animals, and had Beckett's respect.

"Not yet," Nash replied. "Go ahead and get the works done on her." At Beckett's nod of agreement, Nash studied the mare again. "If we can't retrain her, we'll put her into the breeding program." Nash made a name for himself with breeding high quality quarter horses. "She's one of Colby's, and comes from a good line."

Professional bareback bronc rider, Colby Warner, bred quarter horses at his ranch in Wyoming. Any that gave him grief, he sold to Nash for what he'd spent on feed during the horse's upbringing. "Got any videos of her going?"

"A couple. Colby put a few weeks training into her, but said she wasn't worth his trouble. One of his falls was nasty."

Beckett snorted. He knew, as did Nash, that the best horses were ones that had heart. No greater reward than when a man gained the trust of a horse. "Can you send me those videos?"

"I'll add them to your Dropbox when I go back into the house." Callie snatched the finger Nash offered, babbling on like she was right in on the conversation. "Any news on the charges?"

Beckett blew out a frustrated breath. He'd withheld

telling Amelia the news yet, not wanting to ruin her first day back, especially since he figured the last thing she wanted to think about was the dipshit that dumped her at the altar. "As far as I know, Luka is pressing on with the charges. I'm waiting on my lawyer to hear about next steps."

Nash shook his head slowly. "What kind of man can't handle a well-deserved punch?"

"A weak one," Beckett said simply.

Nash agreed with a firm nod. "No matter what happens, you've got a place here for as long as you want it."

"Thanks, man, appreciate that."

Nash gave his classic smart-ass grin and cupped Becketts's shoulder. "Now get to work. I don't pay you to stand around."

Beckett chuckled as Nash strode away and said to Callie, "Now, sweetie, you need to sleep more for your mama."

Beckett's smile faded when he looked back to the mare. Determined to introduce himself to the horse, Beckett headed over to the gate and once through, shut it behind him before facing the mare again. Quarter horses were all Beckett knew growing up. Jefferson Duncan, his grandfather on his mother's side, was a champion calf roper, and Beckett followed in his footsteps for a time. He'd learned the tricks of the trade from his grandfather from the time he was four years old, atop a Shetland pony. He'd even been considered to compete professionally. Until one night changed the direction of his life.

On his way toward the horse, he kept his eyes cast downward, but stayed aware of exactly where the horse was in case she acted aggressively. The mare took a small step back but didn't run when Beckett reached her, offering his hand out for the horse to smell. That feel of warm air brushing against Beckett's hand brought him right back to the fatal car crash that killed Beckett's mother, grandfather and beloved horse, Smokey, all because a trucker fell asleep at the wheel. His mother was pronounced dead at the scene. His grandfather died an hour later in the hospital. Smokey had been euthanized by a state trooper on the side of the road, his injuries too bad to heal. Beckett's life changed after that night. *He* changed after that night. Gone was his dream of becoming a professional calf roper. Not that he didn't love the sport, and wonder what would have been if the accident never happened, but the death of his mother took a hard toll on Beckett's father. Beckett needed to stay close to home.

"Easy," Beckett said, stroking the mare's dark chestnut-colored head.

She snorted once, then took another step back, and Beckett didn't make another move as tires crunched against gravel behind him. He glanced back, finding a white truck and horse trailer driving down the driveway with Black-shaw Training on the side. Two horses that Beckett had trained were off to their new homes.

With a long sigh to ease the mare, he glanced back at his new project, studying her. "Autumn. That'll be your name, sweetheart," he said. Her coloring reminded him of leaves in the fall. Her dark eyes locked onto him. "We're going to do just fine together." As if in agreement, she snorted again, and then he turned away, leaving their first introduction behind them.

Later in the morning, he'd work her in the round pen and get a feel for her, but rushing a troubled horse only led to more problems. He made it back to the gate when his phone in his pocket vibrated. A quick look at the screen revealed it was his lifelong friend, Hayes. "Hey," he answered.

"Mornin'," Hayes said. "Are you working?"

"I'm looking at my new project as we speak," Beckett answered, locking the gate behind him.

A pause. One that always meant trouble.

Hayes' voice tightened. "Listen, I hate to tell you this, but we've got your dad here at the station."

Hayes worked as a detective for the River Rock Police Department. "What's happened?"

"Someone found him passed out drunk in the park this morning."

Beckett shut his eyes and breathed deep before reopening them to Autumn, who still watched Beckett's every move. Yeah, Beckett understood putting up a fight when forced to do things one didn't want to do, and he also understood wanting to give up entirely. He'd been there, more times than he'd like to admit. "Is he hurt?"

"No, just blackout drunk. What do you want us to do with him?"

His father drank only a half dozen times in a year, but when he drank, it never ended well. Though most times, he got inebriated at home, obviously that didn't happen last night. "I'll come get him."

"See you soon," Hayes replied. Then the line went dead.

The world began to press in on Beckett's shoulders as he texted Nash: An emergency has come up. Shoot me those videos. I'll be back in thirty minutes.

Nash replied: Do what you have to do. Sending now.

The sun beat down on Beckett as he shoved his phone back into his pocket, leaving Autumn behind and returning to his truck. His pristine and jacked-up F-150 was his only indulgence.

Back on the road, he took the drive easy, passing by Amelia's place again, finding her driveway empty now. He slid down the window, letting the fresh scents of wildflowers and sunshine take away the tension in his chest.

When he rolled into the downtown, he found the double-lane road quiet. Visitors came for the views of the Colorado mountains, the small town life, and the rich countryside, but the scents of fresh cut grass and clean air were home to Beckett. Along the main street, quaint brick storefronts hugged the thin road. Each store had unique storefronts that had become more modernized over the years.

He parked next to the brown-bricked police station and swiftly entered through the front door, finding Hayes waiting for him in the waiting room. Brown curls peaked out from beneath his friend's black cowboy hat. The tightness of Hayes' amber colored eyes told Beckett his dad was in bad shape. "Thanks for calling."

"Not a problem," Hayes said, gesturing to the door next to the reception desk. "I'll bring you back."

Growing up, Beckett was the last kid who'd end up in a police station. He got good grades, played football and rode in the rodeo, working his way up the rankings. Before the accident, he'd been too busy to get into trouble. After that accident, he'd found trouble often. It seemed that hadn't changed. He'd seen the insides of these walls twice in the last two weeks. Once with his arrest, and now for his father. It didn't feel good, leaving him hypersensitive to the loudness of the voices, banging of fingers typing on keyboards, telephones ringing and the musky smell in the air.

He followed Hayes down the hallway to the back room where the holding cell was located. They passed the cubicles of cops writing up reports or making telephone calls. Every weighted stare only sank more heaviness onto Beckett's shoulders, a firm reminder that he was so far away from living the life he wanted. And no matter how much he'd tried to make things right, he couldn't outrun this part of his life. Though he'd done his best to not become the emotionally crippled man his father had become.

Once they passed through another locked door, a chill ran up his spine. He knew the holding cell personally; he'd been in there the night of Amelia's wedding. He took one look at his father slumped on the thin mattress. A shell of what Jim Stone had once been. "He's still knocked out?"

Hayes nodded, folding his arms. "Like I said, blackout drunk."

Before Beckett's mother died, his father rarely drank, simply enjoying a beer every now and again. After his mother's death, on any day that reminded Jim of his wife, he couldn't survive it and erased the day with booze. Beckett's chest squeezed tight. "Can I take him home?" he asked Hayes.

"Yeah," Hayes said before glancing up at the security camera and nodding.

The cell's door *clicked* open, and Beckett stepped inside. "Dad," he called.

A loud snore greeted him.

"Dad," Beckett said, louder, shaking him on his shoulder.

Jim moaned.

Beckett sighed and glanced back over his shoulders at Hayes. "Sorry, man, but I'm going to need your help getting him home."

Hayes stepped up. "You've got my help. Always."

Beckett would never forget it either. Never forget that even with the hardships and the loss of all his family, the dad he once knew and loved included, he had good friends and a good life that Beckett worked hard to achieve. And now he had the chance to get the one that got away back in his life. Permanently. Keeping that on his mind, and not allowing his father to encroach on Beckett's happiness that Amelia was a free woman again, he grabbed one arm as Hayes grabbed the other. "Dad, wake the hell up."

When they hoisted him up, Jim murmured nonsense.

Every step Beckett took out of the cell made him proud that, after he lost his way when his mother and grandfather died, he eventually found his way back to himself. Sure, he'd fallen deeper into a pit of misery when Amelia fell in love with someone else, but seeing her leave had been the push to better himself. It had made him look hard at himself and question why he let her walk out of his life, and it had made him realize she did deserve better than him. It made him change. Do better. Be better. And as they headed out of the police station, he promised himself that he'd get everything right this time around.

## 3

A fter a round of texts with Luka, Amelia parked her bright blue Yaris at the curb in downtown River Rock, the hard lump still stuck in her throat. The very last thing she wanted to do was face Luka, but no way would she let Beckett take the fall for the mess she'd caused. She kept her head down, feeling watchful stares from the locals. No doubt they wanted to give their condolences, like her life was over. Dammit, her life wasn't over, not even close. On her honeymoon, and after a much-deserved emotional breakdown, she'd discovered a newfound steadiness inside herself. She would live her life on her terms. She had a clear head, and she was determined to listen to her heart instead of stuffing all her emotions deep down and ignoring them. And her heart was telling her that she needed to do this for Beckett, no matter how much she wanted to turn and run far away from Luka.

She crossed the road, approaching the signage that read: HOT BREW AND EATS. The local coffee shop made a killer pumpkin spiced latte in the fall and a chocolate fudge brownie to die for all year long. When she entered the brown-bricked building, she found the shop quiet this morning, only a few customers sitting around the retro-style booths finished in brown leather. In one of those booths sat Luka. He caught her arrival and gave her a small, pathetic smile, which she didn't return. Instead, she headed for the counter. "Hey Betty," she said, reaching the twenty-something woman with the big brown eyes. "Can I get a vanilla latte?" She'd gone to high school with Betty's older sister.

"Sure. That'll be three sixty-five," Betty said, giving a sweet as sugar smile. "I told him that *he* wasn't welcome here, but he said you were meeting him. That's the only reason his sorry ass is still in the shop."

Amelia laughed softly, taking out her debit card. "Thanks for sticking up for me, but yeah, I asked him to meet me here." Even the locals in the booths around the shop were giving Amelia a warm smile, then proceeded to give Luka the stink eye. He was the city guy out of Denver who'd broken the heart of a River Rock native. No one would welcome him back. Amelia cursed the part of her heart, albeit a small part, that felt bad for him.

Betty typed the amount into the debit machine. "If that changes, let me know, and I'll kick him outta here."

"Thanks, Betty. I appreciate it." Amelia tapped her card against the machine, waiting for the beep before she slid her card back into her wallet. "Do you mind bringing my drink over when it's ready?"

"Not at all. It'll just be a minute."

Amelia sent her another grateful smile both for the latte and the protection, and then she did the one thing she didn't want to do; she approached Luka. His gaze remained glued to her every step. His expression uneasy. He didn't rise when she sidled up to the table, something he never did when a woman approached a table. Something River Rock men always did. It occurred to her now how much that used to bother her about Luka. She wondered when she'd stopped caring that he had terrible manners.

"Hi," she said, sliding into the booth in front of him. Only then did she get a good look at him, and she cringed. "Your face looks terrible." His nose definitely had been broken. The middle now had a dent in it, and he was sporting two black eyes.

"My face feels terrible," Luka grumbled, fiddling with the to-go mug. His voice didn't sound quite right either, more nasally.

Betty approached the table. She set Amelia's latte down in the front of her and said to her, "Enjoy." To Luka, she snapped, "I hope you choke on your drink."

Amelia fought her smile as Betty whirled and headed back to the counter.

Luka sighed. "Everyone here hates me."

"Are you surprised?" Amelia asked, glancing his way again, finding his head bowed.

He shrugged. "Not really."

She took in the slump of his shoulders and the heaviness in his voice, and her heart reached for him, even though she knew it shouldn't. For the last two weeks, she'd been living it up, healing her heart with pina coladas and sunshine by the ocean. He'd obviously been in a living hell. She could only imagine the fury of his mother at wasting her hard-earned money on a wedding that never happened. And the embarrassment she must have endured within her catty group of friends. She really didn't want to punish him further. "I didn't ask you to come here to hash everything out or to make you feel bad or anything like that."

His head lifted, surprise glinting on his face. "You don't want to talk about what happened?"

"Actually, no I don't," she said, a revelation to herself too.

"I don't want to relive everything that happened. We were something. Now we're nothing."

Tears welled in his eyes before he looked down to his coffee cup and composed himself. "I wish I would have done—"

"Stop." He snapped his gaze to hers, and she sighed. "Please just stop. I left River Rock heartbroken. I don't feel heartbroken anymore. I feel raw, but okay. I don't want apologies. I want to move on with my life."

His head cocked, curiosity brimming in his eyes. "Then why did you call me here?"

To shake off the confusing, pitying emotion she did feel for Luka, and the slight fear that she had no clue what would happen from this day forward, she took a long sip of her latte, glad for the warmth the drink sent into her bones. "To talk about the charges that you filed against Beckett," she eventually said.

Luka's expression changed in a flash, all the sadness turning into something vengeful. "There's nothing to talk about. The charges have nothing to do with you."

"It certainly feels like it has something to do with me," she countered, setting her drink down in front of her. "Not only did you end our engagement in the most spectacularly cruel way, but now you're dragging all this out by charging one of my friends with assault."

Luka pointed to his nose. "Look at what he did to my face, Amelia."

She cringed. "Yeah, I see what he did. It's bad." Maisie had said that Beckett had knocked Luka out cold, but Amelia hadn't stuck around to find out. She'd run out of the brewery and locked herself in the bathroom until everyone left. "But not as bad as what you did to my heart."

Luka blew out a frustrated breath. He scraped a hand

across his face, then groaned when his fingers reached his black eye. "I'm sorry for breaking your heart."

Her whole plan wasn't to go there, but her heart suddenly demanded an answer. "Are you sorry? Truly sorry?"

"Yes, of course, I'm sorry." He set those puppy dog eyes on her that she once loved having look her way. Her heart squeezed, but not as much as she expected, as he said, "But come on, you must have known that something wasn't right with us. We just got stuck in the idea of a wedding. It can't just be me. We haven't been happy for a while. All we did was argue. I saved us from a nasty divorce down the road."

"You saved us?" she asked, incredulous. "Oh, well, thank you very much for being so considerate for saving me from being hurt further by dumping me at the altar."

He sighed. "You know what I mean."

"Actually, what I do know is that you think you know what's best for me. And you most certainly don't, because if you did, you wouldn't have embarrassed me in front of all my family and friends."

"My family was there too."

"That makes what you did better?" She drew in a deep breath, her insides shaking, which was exactly what she didn't want. She let out a slow, deep breath, cooling the heat boiling in her blood. "I don't want to do this. We're never going to find a resolution, because what you did was cruel even though you thought it was the right thing to do." She took another long sip of her drink, steadying her hand, shoving all the hot rage away. "Again, this isn't why I called you here. I don't want to talk about us, about what happened, about anything."

"Then what do you want?" Luka asked, coldly.

"I want you to drop the charges against Beckett."

He shook his head firmly. "I can't do that."

She fisted her hands on the table. "Why? Pride? Did Beckett make you feel small in front of all your family?"

"No," Luka said with a loud snort. "I need to fix what he did to my fucking nose, Amelia. My insurance only covered the original break. When it healed, it looked like this." He pointed to his nose. "The surgery costs ten grand to make it look normal again. I don't have that kind of money lying around after paying for the wedding. Look at me. I can't leave my nose like this."

*Oh.* "Well, did you ask Beckett to pay for the surgery?"

"I did. He refused."

She sighed. Of course, he did. "You deserved that punch, Luka, whether you want to own up to that or not," she said, loudly, over the grinding of the coffee beans. A rich nutty aroma infused the air as she continued, "Sending a good man to jail because you broke my heart into a million pieces for all to see is wrong."

Luka glanced back down to his paper cup and gave a small shrug. "He's gotta pay for the surgery. I'm not going into debt because he broke my fucking nose."

Amelia paused, drawing in the deepest breath of her life, determined to put all this behind her and to get a fresh start. "Ten thousand, that's what you need for the surgery?"

Luka's gaze met hers. "Yeah."

Amelia rose, taking her latte with her. "I'll courier the check to your house tomorrow morning. I expect you to drop the charges after you receive the money. Got it?"

"I'm not going to take ten grand from you," Luka said, adamant.

"Actually, you are," she snapped, glaring at him. "Because you owe me this. After the shit you've pulled, you will do this and let this go so I can move on with my life."

Luka paused, hot jealously flaring on his expression. "Why are you doing this for *him*?"

Before she turned away from Luka forever, she said, "I put Beckett into this situation because I brought you into our lives. He was protecting *me*. Now it's my turn to protect him."

֍

"DAD, YOU COULD HELP A LITTLE," Beckett groaned, holding half of his father's weight as he helped him up the rickety old porch steps of his childhood home that was located on the cusp of his grandfather's land. The Duncans had once owned two hundred acres of pristine Colorado countryside. When his grandfather passed, he left the land to Beckett's mother, which transferred to his father after the accident. Jim had sold all the land, except for the ten acres around the house. But on the east side of the land, alongside a babbling creek, Beckett inherited his grandfather's ranch style farm-house and the horse farm, along with the fifty acres surrounding the property. That land would remain Beckett's for as long as he was alive, in honor of his grandfather. He'd moved into the property the day after he turned eighteen years old, and the farm officially became his under the estate.

Hayes grunted on the other side of Jim. "How is he still this drunk?"

"It's a talent," Beckett grumbled, awkwardly holding his father while using his key to open the front door of his child-hood home.

They staggered through the door, and Beckett inhaled the familiar scents around him. A little dusty, a bit damp, all that was missing was the aromas coming from the kitchen of his mother baking something delicious for him to eat. He left the front door wide open. His childhood cat that would have once escaped had passed a few years ago at the age of twenty-seven. Nothing in this house was as it once was, the emptiness was near suffocating.

By the time they set Jim into the recliner in front of the television in the small living room, Beckett was breathing heavily and sweating. He grabbed his dad's shirt and adjusted him in the chair before flipping the leg rest up. His dad's snores followed.

"Will he be all right here?" Hayes asked.

"Yeah, he'll be all right. I'll check in on him later." Beckett grabbed the blanket off the back of the couch, and after removing his dad's shoes, his set the blanket over him. There were things Beckett knew for certain. One, his father's life drastically changed when his wife died in that accident that altered all their lives forever. Two, he never recovered from his pain. And Beckett, without a doubt in his mind, would never be like him. His pain was always there, but the heavy loss of his mother and grandfather wasn't the driving force of his life. At least not anymore, after years of therapy and the will to better his life.

He'd tried for years to save his father. But when Beckett realized he hadn't followed Amelia to Denver, and he'd given up his dreams of becoming a professional calf roper, all because he needed to stay in town and be close to his father to watch out for him, he knew he had to stop. He loved his father, but he quit hurting his life to better his father's.

Hayes followed Beckett back outside, and as Beckett relocked the front door, Hayes asked, "Any idea what spurred this?"

"Yesterday was my mother's birthday," Beckett said, trotting down the porch steps and hoping back into his truck, fastening his seatbelt.

"Shit," said Hayes, when he slid into the seat next to him. "I totally forgot. You all right, man?"

Beckett nodded, turning on his truck and reversing out of

the driveway. "I'm not in the same headspace as him. Yeah, I miss her, but not living isn't going to bring her back."

Hayes agreed with a swift nod, fastening his seatbelt. "Good headspace to have."

Beckett settled his wrist atop the steering wheel, the truck's engine humming as he drove Hayes back into town. "Is my dad looking at any charges?"

Hayes shook his head. "Nah, he wasn't being a nuisance, just an eyesore to those in the park."

Beckett hadn't felt embarrassed over his father in a long time. The town knew his dad, knew his history, and knew that sometimes Jim fell apart. Beckett had been well on his way to becoming that same guy. Until his mind cleared and healing began, and while he had wished the same healing for his father, Beckett eventually accepted, with the help of therapy, that was never going to happen. Determined to keep his promise to never again allow his father to ruin his day, he shifted the conversation. "Did you hear Amelia's back?"

"Yeah, I did," Hayes said, tension in his voice.

Beckett gave him a quick look. "What is it?"

Hayes' lips pinched before he glanced sidelong. "Amelia was in town meeting with Luka."

Beckett swerved the truck to the side of the road and slammed on the brakes, dust bellowing around them. "Say that again?"

Hayes removed his hand from the dash he'd obviously been holding to avoid slamming into it. "I told Maisie you wouldn't be happy about this, but when do any of the Carter sisters listen to me?"

Only one thing mattered to Beckett. "Is she getting back together with him?"

"That's a negative," Hayes said with a snort, leaning his elbow against the open window. "Maisie said there's absolutely no chance of that."

"Thank God," Beckett breathed, slowly his racing heart. "That prick doesn't deserve her."

"No, he doesn't."

Beckett glanced out the front window, realizing he pulled off outside his house. From the road, the quaint but gorgeously built ranch farmhouse stood proud atop a small hill. The barn with the five horse stables was to the right. The property had four large paddocks, with a sand ring and round pen that his grandfather used during his rodeo career. Beckett knew that's why his grandfather left him the property in his will and didn't gift it to his mother. Back then, Beckett was meant to follow in his footsteps. Even if Beckett wasn't using the stables or fields, he kept the property in pristine condition and he never stopped training with his rope. He still loved the sport, missed it every day, but he knew he would never go pro. He let out a long sigh, considering what he heard. "If Amelia is not meeting him to reconnect, why is she seeing him?"

"Yeah, this is the part you're not going to like," Hayes grumbled. "Darryl and Penelope popped over to her house this morning with groceries. Maisie told me that they updated her on what transpired between you and Luka."

"And somehow, *that* made Amelia want to meet up with that fuckhead?" Christ, Beckett had only *just* seen her again.

"From what Maisie's told me, she's doing it to protect you."

Beckett went still. "Protect me from what exactly?"

"Jail time."

Beckett's hand tightened around the steering wheel. He didn't have to look to know his knuckles were white. "Where is he?"

Hayes gave him a firm look. The cop, at the ready. "Get that idea out of your head. You can't go see him. He's got a restraining order." Unusual softness reached Hayes' gaze as he shifted in his seat and cupped Beckett's shoulder. "Besides, what's done is done, there is nothing you can do now anyway."

That fire burning in his gut began to creep up his face. "What do you mean, what's done is done?"

"Apparently, Amelia paid off Luka for the surgery to make this all go away."

Beckett's vision tunneled. He thrust his hands into his hair, desperately trying to hold onto his damn pride. "What in the hell was she thinking?"

"It's not hard to imagine how responsible she'd feel for this. That she'd want to protect you."

Beckett dropped his head back against his head rest and breathed deep. "I didn't want to pay that fucker off."

Hayes chuckled. "He did look good sporting that nose."

Beckett slid his glanced sideways and gave a grin he doubted looked amused. "He did."

A long moment passed as a tractor drove by, the slight breeze carrying the fresh scents of timothy hay in his neighbor's fields. On one hand, rage simmered that she'd pay that prick off. On the other hand, he liked her jumping in to save him from jail time. It gave him hope that somehow, someway, he'd win her back and she'd never know what a broken heart felt like again.

"So," Hayes eventually said, breaking the silence. "What's the plan now?"

Beckett looked his way with an arched eyebrow. "With Amelia?"

"Yeah."

Beckett focused back on his house. So many wonderful memories were held there. All the hours Amelia spent watching Beckett as he trained for the rodeo under his grandfather's guidance. All the rides they'd gone on, exploring the Duncan land on horseback. His gaze found the barn, the hayloft being the very spot that Beckett had taken Amelia's virginity. Knowing there was nothing he wouldn't do now to get her back in this house with him, he grinned at Hayes. "I hope she throat punches that asshole, and then I'm going to give her hell for paying a debt that belonged to me."

Hayes laughed. "Sounds like a damn good plan to me."

## 4

After Amelia arrived back home, the lingering tension of meeting Luka followed her. She skipped the house and went straight for the brewery, needing to figure out a plan on getting it back into shape. With every step she took, she kept waiting for her heart to squeeze tight, missing Luka, to feel more broken, raw, *anything*, but she only felt glad to keep Beckett from facing jail time. And something about that kept rubbing her wrong. She'd spent nearly three years with Luka, why wasn't she trying to understand why he ended things so cruelly? Why didn't she want an explanation from him? Why wasn't she ready to let him have it and to feel the pain he'd put her through? She amounted this to getting over the worst of her heartbreak in the tropics. But there was this little part of her heart that told her there was a good chance that Luka should have been in her rearview mirror for a long time, and maybe the reason she couldn't hate him for what he'd done was because, beyond the embarrassment and the sadness that the life she dreamed up was over, maybe the life she thought she had with Luka wasn't real to begin with.

When she reached for the first tank, she noted the pungent smell in the brewery had improved greatly with the barn doors left open for most of the morning. The dust begrudgingly hadn't improved. First thing first, the tanks needed cleaning.

She only got one step into the barn, when from behind her, Beckett snapped, "What did you do?"

Whirling around, she found Beckett's face tight and muscles straining. The one bad thing about small towns was word got around fast, and obviously, he'd learned about her meeting Luka today. Trying to play dumb to avoid the conversation she didn't want to have, she turned back to her work. "I'm about to clean my tanks," she said.

His voice tightened. "That is not the answer to my question, and you know it."

She refused to look back, hearing the anger in his low voice, and not wanting to see it on his face. "I did what had to be done," she told him. To keep her hands busy, she reached for a cloth and began dusting along the stairs that led up to the top of the tank.

"That payment was mine to make, Amelia, not yours," he said, his voice barely controlled. "If you had asked me, I would have told you that I rejected his offer to pay him because I don't want the prick to fix his nose. He should wear that shame for the rest of his life."

She'd never missed pina coladas on the beach more than she did right now. With a heavy sigh, she turned to face Beckett, spotting the vein in the middle of his head bulging like it would burst any second. Of course, she had expected him to show up, but she wasn't expecting his anger. But it didn't matter, she wanted this behind her. For good. "What is bothering you the most here, Beckett: that *I* paid to fix your problem or that Luka will get his nose fixed?"

Beckett arched an eyebrow. "Do I need to pick one? Can't both piss me off equally?"

A laugh nearly escaped her, but nothing about any of this was funny. She knew all too well that fate was not in her hands. The death of her parents taught her that. But she didn't need to sit by and let fate decide everything without fighting back either. "What did you expect me to do?" she countered, glaring at him. "Let you go to jail for me?"

To anyone else, he'd look intimidating with his legs planted wide and his nostrils flaring, but she heard the warmth in his voice behind the tightness as he said, "I expect for you to come and talk to me about it, instead of giving that bastard your money."

Yeah, well, she could play the intimidating part too. She flatted her lips, placing her hands on her hips. "You never would have agreed to pay him if I'd asked you."

"You're damn right I wouldn't have," he growled, his face reddening.

Heat flushed through her body as she ground her teeth, turning away from him. God, he'd always been a hard wall that she'd beat her head against. But she realized in this moment that her arguments were so different with Beckett than they were with Luka. Luka got upset when she wouldn't change something about herself for him. Beckett only ever got upset when he felt she was treated wrongly. Her stomach roiled in awareness that she'd forgotten what it was like to have someone support her. "Well, it's done and over and now we can all put this behind us and move on."

"Don't kid yourself, Amelia. Nothing is behind us," he said slowly and coldly, flicking her gaze to him. His look was all knowing. "You can't simply brush this under a rug and hope it all goes away."

"Why not?" she asked, throwing up in hands in frustration. "Why can't I pay Luka off and end this entire shitshow? What is the harm in that?"

Beckett's expression softened. A smidgen. "The harm is that you caved when you shouldn't have."

Her chest heaved, breathing become rough and rapid. "I caved to protect you."

A gust of wind swept up dirt up around him as he crossed his arms, his brows knotting. "I didn't ask you to do that. If I had wanted to pay the asshole off, I would have fucking paid him."

"Yeah, right." She snorted. "You have too much pride for that."

"This has nothing to do with pride," he snapped, reaching into his back pocket. "This was my problem. Not yours." He offered her a check. "I won't pay him, but I will pay you. Take it."

"No," she said, firmly. "My problem, not yours."

His eyes slowly narrowed into slits. "Amelia."

Her gut began to boil. She'd had about enough of men today. She tossed the cloth down on the stairs and closed the distance between them, getting into his space. "I get you're pissed, really I do, but can't you just say thank you and be done with it?"

A laughter with an edge escaped him. "Do tell me what I should be thanking you for."

She was pushing him. She knew it. She also wasn't about to back down. "For making this all go away. For ensuring that you wouldn't get jail time. For protecting you like you protected me when your fist hit Luka's face."

A pause. His gaze flared. "I will never thank you for that."

She stared him down, and he glared right back for many, *many* seconds. Years they'd been together, and from those years, she knew that he wouldn't give, not when it came to protecting someone he cared about. The silence drudged on

44

until she threw her hands up. "Honestly, Beckett, you'll have to explain this to me. Why are you so mad?"

Intensity simmered on his face as he closed the distance between them, bringing the hard wall of his chest nearly against hers. She felt the heat emanating off him and was shocked when her nipples puckered in response to him being this close. Tingles raced through her all the way to the tips of her toes as he said, tightly, "I'm mad about all of it. I'm mad that you left for college, and I was too much of a fucking mess to go with you. I'm mad that you met that fucker, and he got his damn claws into you. I'm mad that instead of you being blissfully happy, I watched your heart shatter before my eyes." His chin dipped, bringing his mouth near inches from hers, his warm breath brushing across her face. "I'm mad that instead of that prick suffering, he has *your* fucking money to fix his stupid face. And I'm mad that I have no way to stop any of it."

The world narrowed on him with each and every meaningful word that passed his mouth. The affection, the protection, the sheer helplessness, all affected her in a way she never anticipated feeling again. She became tangled in the safe energy he projected. The familiarly of having him close. She took in his simmering eyes with so much emotion in them she could barely breathe. The heat of his body, the strength of him, so close to her. His sculpted lips drew her in, closer and closer, until her hands fisted his T-shirt and her mouth met his.

Beckett stiffened. He did not return the kiss.

At the coldness against her mouth, she gasped and broke away, horror making her blood run cold. "Oh my God, Beckett, I'm so sorry."

Only silence greeted her. Was he shaking?

His eyebrow slowly arched. "Did you do that to shut me up or because you wanted to kiss me?"

Heat crept over her face. "I don't know why I did that." She swallowed deeply, and then began rambling, "No that's not true. I was just thinking how nice it felt to have someone protecting me and caring about me... and it seemed familiar and safe... and your mouth looked good..."

More silence descended. Until all the shock on Beckett's face was swept away to reveal raw, unadulterated lust, an expression she hadn't seen from him for a very long time. It occurred to her then she missed being looked at like that – with fierce hunger. Like no other woman compared to her. Like he didn't care what hell he had to walk through to reach her, he'd do it time and time again. Like he was just the reckless kid that wanted something and didn't care what the consequences cost him.

She wanted to be that person she was back then with him. The one who didn't know what heartbreak felt like. The one who laughed often and believed anything was possible. She swallowed again, swearing her heart was beating loud enough for both of them to hear.

A beat.

Then a gasp ripped from her throat as he grabbed the front of her shirt and yanked her against the hard planes of his body. He did what she didn't do. He finished the kiss.

A moment later, her back hit the beer tank, and Beckett wasted no time devouring her neck with his hot kisses. She pushed off his cowboy hat to run her hands through his hair, feeling her sane mind unravel at his passion. Her mind shut off and only her body was thinking now. Beckett's touch was imprinted on her skin, reminding her of teenage freedom and wild affection.

"Ew, my eyes," Maisie screamed.

Amelia broke away from Beckett with a loud gasp, snapping her eyes open, finding her sisters standing in the barn's open double doors. Maisie was blinking rapidly, and Clara's back was ramrod straight. Amelia stared at them for a second before they both turned and walked away.

Beckett chuckled proudly. But Amelia wasn't laughing at what her sisters had caught her doing two weeks after she was dumped at the altar. "There is something wrong with me," Amelia muttered. "Seriously, something wrong with me. I can't believe I just kissed you like that. I'm sorry, Beckett. Please forgive me."

Right as she raised her shaky hands to cover her face, Beckett grabbed her wrists. "There's nothing wrong with you," he stated. The kiss he dropped on her mouth was indecent and the best kiss of her entire life. He gave her a panty-melting smirk. "Just to clarify, I'm not one bit sorry about that kiss."

When he released her, she wobbled. Sure, back when they dated, Beckett had always known how to make her blush and kiss her just right, but this was a man's kiss, not the kiss of a kid looking for some fun. This kiss had intent, power, and made her hunger to taste it again.

Before she could even think straight, he was striding past her sisters, giving them a simple hello like what they'd walked in on was everyday business.

Clara whirled around to Amelia, her eyes huge and mouth gaping open. She appeared to try to talk, but nothing was coming out.

Maisie gave a shit-eating grin. "If that's not a spectacular welcome home, I don't know what is."

## 5

---

**B**eckett couldn't fight the smile on his face, even if he and Amelia had been interrupted. He'd waited years to touch her again. When she'd kissed him, he'd been so shocked it had taken him a moment to catch up. But one look into her pretty eyes filled with desire, albeit mixed with confusion, and he was a goner. Yeah, this would happen on her terms, but he was one hundred percent there for whatever she wanted from him, whenever she wanted him, until he could win her heart back and keep her at his side forever.

Not wanting to make Amelia any more uncomfortable than she already looked at her sisters' arrival, he'd left to give her space and avoid an awkward conversation he was certain she did not want to have with him there. Later, he'd finish what they started today, and ensure she felt good about it all, but that wasn't going to happen with her hovering sisters.

When he reached his truck, Clara called from behind him, "Hold up, Beckett." He sighed. On good days, Clara was tough and had sharp claws. Beckett doubted Clara would consider this a good day. Against his better judgement, he turned to her. "Hello, Clara."

She stopped in front of her, her face scrunched. "You shouldn't have done that."

He stared into Clara's hard blue eyes, knowing her fierceness came from a deep love for Amelia. They'd always been incredibly close. But he didn't owe her jack shit. "I know you're worried about your sister, and rightly so, but what happens with Amelia is between us."

Clara's eyes slowly narrowed. "You do realize she just had her heart broken, right?"

"Yes, I'm well aware."

She lifted her chin, crossing her arms. "You also realize that you once obliterated her heart too, right?"

His chest felt the hit, and he deserved the blow. "I've never forgotten what I've done to her."

"Good. I'm glad to hear that." Her nostrils flared as she closed in on him, pointing at his face. "Do not hurt her, Beckett. I'll kill you myself if you do."

Beckett wouldn't put it past her, either. And he knew the Carter sisters were smart enough to get away with murder too.

"Stop it," Amelia snapped.

Clara whirled around to her sister and gasped, "Amelia—"

"Just stop," Amelia said, softer now. Her gaze flicked at Beckett's, steady and strong. "Come back after work, okay?"

"I'll be here." He slid his gaze to Clara again. Her breathing was heavy, her teeth nearly bared. Not in all the years he'd known this family had he ever seen her so mad, but he wouldn't apologize for kissing Amelia today. And he wouldn't apologize for kissing her later when he came back if she wanted that too.

A second later, he was back in his truck, spotting all three sisters watching him as he drove out of the driveway. He whistled to himself, knowing he might very well be a dead man walking. Yet death was worth it. For years he'd waited to have Amelia again. To taste her. To smell that vanilla scent she carried. Now that he had it all again, he only wanted more, and so did his hard cock. But he wasn't foolish enough to know that he walked on emotional territory here. Two weeks ago, she had planned to marry someone else, but deep down, he'd hoped she realized that wedding didn't happen because she was meant for Beckett, not that prick. As the truck hit a pothole in the road, Beckett realized that first, he needed to gain her trust and her friendship again to let her heart reopen to him, and if she wanted to kiss him while that happened, he'd never stop her.

Determined to get his day moving ahead, he slowed at a stop sign and quickly dialed Dr. Alan. The receptionist, Shelby, answered on the second ring. "Hey, this is Beckett. Is Dr. Alan around our area today? I need a horse looked over before we get into training."

"Hi, Beckett," she said, her voice bubbly. "Dr. Alan is actually just leaving the Blackshaw Guest Ranch now. Want me to send him your way?"

"Please do," Beckett said. "Thanks, Shelby."

"No problem. Bye."

The phone call ended, and the country music radio station sprang to life through his speakers. Beckett rolled down his window, letting the air cool his overheated flesh. His thoughts desperately wanted to return to Amelia's sweet and ripe body, but he forced himself to think of the mare and her challenges.

When he reached the farm, it pleased him to see the vet driving up the driveway behind him. Beckett parked next to the paddock where Autumn lived for now. Eventually she'd go out in a small herd. Dr. Alan, with the River Rock Veterinary Clinic logo on the side of his van, parked next to him.

"Hey," Beckett said when he reached Dr. Alan and his assistant at the hood of their van.

"What do you have for me today?" Dr. Alan asked. He was an astute man, in his late seventies, a face full of wrinkles and wisdom.

"This girl here," Beckett said, moving to the gate. He grabbed the halter and lead, and Autumn didn't put up a fuss when he slid the halter over her head.

"Seems well-mannered on the ground," Dr. Alan said, studying the mare. "What's the problem exactly?"

Most horses that came through the farm had bad attitudes. The worst of the worst. And Dr. Alan was well aware of that fact. "She's pure sugar until someone gets on her back, then she's all sour."

Dr. Alan chuckled before his expression fell, becoming serious again. Like it did every time he came to give his advice on a horse. Beckett held the lead chank but stayed out of the way as Dr. Alan ran through his examination, alongside his assistant.

By the time Dr. Alan finished, the mare's ears were pinned back, obviously sick of the flexion tests and all the other poking and prodding she went through. "She's got some back pain, which I suspect might be from an ill-fitting saddle." He rubbed at her withers where white hair was located on the right side, indicating trauma where the saddle fit. "Other than that, I'm not seeing anything medically wrong which would be causing her behavior."

"All clear to work then?" Beckett asked.

Dr. Alan nodded. "Yes, I'm good with that recommendation."

"Great," Beckett said. "Thanks for coming out."

"Always a pleasure," Dr. Alan said, before heading back to his van.

Beckett turned his attention to Autumn and gave her face

a caress. "No excuses now sweetheart. We'll get the saddle right and get you going."

The horse snorted, pushing off his hand from her face.

"Not that easy, huh?" Beckett chuckled, removing the halter and letting the horse back out to graze to give her a break before he started to work with her.

As he walked back to the gate, tires crunching against gravel lifted his attention to the driveway. Sullivan drove up in his truck. Sullivan might be Beckett's other closest buddy, but he was also Clara's husband. Beckett shouldn't have been surprised that Clara sent Sullivan his way.

"She's gorgeous," Sullivan said the moment he got out of the truck. Sullivan spent his teenage summers working for the Blackshaw ranch. Now he was a professional baseball player who signed with the Red Sox. He and Clara lived in River Rock for as much time as they could with their son, Mason, but during the summers they lived in Boston and came back to River Rock whenever Sullivan had time off from training or games, even if they only stayed a couple days.

Beckett closed the gate behind him. "She might be gorgeous, but she's dirty."

Sullivan smiled, leaning against the fence. "Sounds like fun."

"Should be interesting." Beckett sidled next to him, resting his arms against the top railing. "I'm guessing you're not here to talk about the horse."

Sullivan gave a dry laugh, glancing sidelong at him. "Clara suggested that I come and see you and have a chat, so I'm here to say I've been here and talked with you."

Beckett chuckled, looking back at the mare who ate grass but kept an eye on him. "I haven't seen her that pissed in my life." Clara was a force. One he didn't want coming after him.

"Pissed might be an understatement, my friend," Sullivan

said with a sly smile before that smile fell. "She's worried about Amelia. That's all."

"I can appreciate that," Beckett said. "In all fairness, I questioned her sanity too when she grabbed me and kissed the hell out of me."

Sullivan cocked his head. "Oh, yeah?"

Hayes and Sullivan were more than friends, they were Beckett's family. No secrets came between them. "I'm not gonna say I didn't hesitate, but I sure as hell wasn't going to stop her."

Sullivan hesitated. "Tell me if I'm stepping in it and you want me out of it, but is this particularly wise?"

"Probably not," Beckett replied honestly. "But I've done the quiet thing. I stayed silent when she went off to college, so she could chase her dreams. I stayed silent when she came back with that prick. I even stayed quiet when she was going to marry him. I'm done sitting back doing nothing. I want her, Sullivan. Just her. If she wants me back, then that's the greatest thing to ever happen to me."

Softness reached Sullivan's expression as he cupped Beckett's shoulder. "Then don't let anything stand in your way, brother." He gave a sly smile. "Not even two overprotective and loud sisters."

&

AFTER BECKETT'S truck disappeared down the driveway, Amelia trotted up the porch steps, feeling her sisters hot on her heels, confusion swirling in her head. The last thing she thought of doing this morning was kissing Beckett. Considering she was dumped at the altar two weeks ago, the last thing Amelia should be thinking about is kissing anyone. Especially Beckett, a man she had history with, and yet, she couldn't find any regret anywhere within her. And *that* was confusing.

"What in the holy hell was that?" Clara asked, following Amelia into the house. The door slammed closed behind them.

"I really don't think I need to explain it," Amelia replied, moving straight to the liquor cabinet next to the pantry. She took out a shot glass and the whiskey, downing the shot immediately to ease the trembling in her insides. Residual adrenaline from the rush of being with Beckett. Was this what happened when a woman had a complete mental breakdown?

"I'd also like to hear you try to explain what we walked in on." Maisie laughed, taking a seat at the kitchen table.

"This isn't funny, Maisie," Clara snapped.

"Oh, please, it's a little funny," Maisie countered. "Besides, they both looked happy. What is so wrong with that?"

Amelia glanced over her shoulder at her little sister and threw her a grateful smile. The whiskey burned down her throat, and she considered having another shot to kill the remaining quivers in her belly that only had a little to do with shock, but she had a lot of work to do today, so she sealed up the bottle. She repeated what Clara had asked over and over again in her mind: *What in the holy hell was that?* Even Amelia had no idea. She'd never acted so boldly or so out of character.

Feeling more stable, she sighed, glancing back at her sisters. "You're worried about me. I get it, but I'm fine."

"How can you be fine?" Clara asked, arms folded over her chest, looking much like a scolding mother in her dress pants, frilly pink blouse and gorgeous black heels.

"Easy," Amelia replied. "It turns out two weeks in the tropics and a whole lot of fun can do wonders for a broken heart."

"I sure bet it does," Maisie said with a grin.

Clara still grimaced. "Amelia—"

"Clara, please just stop." Her voice came out harsher than she intended. She closed in on her older sister, her very best friend. "I'm only going to say this once, so please hear me. I don't need you to meddle in this. I'm not even sure what happened between me and Beckett, but he is, and always has been, a good guy. For some reason, today I grabbed him and kissed him. I started this. So, please let me figure out why in the hell I did that. Okay?"

Clara's eyes searched Amelia's for a long moment until she heaved a sigh, and suddenly, everything hard about her went soft. "Okay, Amelia. I hear you. I'm just protective, and I'm really worried that you're not thinking straight."

"I know you are, and I love you for it." Especially because Amelia wasn't sure she was thinking straight either. She'd loved Luka and had planned a future with him. Beckett was her past, and yet today it hadn't felt that way at all. She kissed Clara's cheek, hoping to put an end to this conversation. "If I feel lost or need advice, you'll be the first one I'll call." Done with talking about all this until she got her head straight about it all, she moved on. "Now, how about we talk about more important things, like my visit with Ronnie this morning."

Clara headed for the coffee pot and took out the filters from the cupboard. "He texted me this morning to let me know that you'd reached out about a meeting."

"I felt bad for leaving so abruptly," Amelia explained, taking the chair across from Maisie at the table. "But he seemed all right with it all."

"Of course he would be understanding," Maisie said, her hair done in a side fishtail braid today, and her jean overalls covered in paint. She'd obviously come from the art studio she owned downtown. "I mean, if he wasn't, what kind of jackass would he be?"

"A big one." Amelia nodded agreement. "So, the marketing department came up with a brilliant idea." She caught her sisters up on all that happened with Ronnie this morning and his idea for the sample beers throughout the year. "Basically, all I need to do is come up with a half dozen samples for them to choose from, beat out the other breweries competing, and we've got the next big push we've been looking for."

"That's an incredible opportunity," Clara said, leaning against the counter while the coffee brewed behind her. "It's amazing how much they're pushing the brewery for us."

"Truly," Amelia agreed. "He's really pulling for us." She couldn't have dreamt this up when she finished the Beer Industry Program at the university of Denver. Many of her classmates never got their beer into distribution, typically selling only locally. For Amelia that would have been fine, but Clara being the business minded one, always saw the bigger picture and drove the brewery to the success it had now. Maisie was artsy, and she got out of the brewery business nearly as quick as she got into it, but she lived out her dreams in her art studio. "Things are a little bit in disarray," Amelia said to Clara, "but I'll get the brewery back up and running smoothly soon enough. Then I'll get started on the samples once I get some more Foxy Diva brewing."

"Excellent news," Clara said, pride glistening in her eyes. "Let me know if you need any help from me."

Amelia nodded. "Will do." Those were empty words. Clara had already done so much for the company. Handling the beer and the brewery fell onto Amelia's shoulders, and she wanted to prove she could keep up her end of the deal.

Maisie said, "You know I'd offer to help, but I'll make more of a mess."

Amelia laughed. "You will, so thanks, I'll pass on the help."

Maisie chuckled and shrugged it off. She was the best artist that Amelia knew, but that was her wheelhouse, absolutely nothing else. She still did her part for the brewery by designing any new logos or graphics for the company, and whenever a big event came around, Maisie helped out. Every time.

Amelia added, "The only downside in all this is if I don't come up with amazing samples, we lose the spot."

Clara's eyes searched Amelia's for a long moment. "It's a lot of pressure to put on you. Are you ready for this? No one is going to be upset if this is too much too soon, Amelia."

"I'm ready," she lied.

Maisie asked, "Do you have any ideas yet?"

*No.* Amelia forced a smile. "I'm working on them." She'd never admit that she had absolutely no ideas at all. Her creative juices felt drained dry. Sure, she had some old ideas in her notebooks of ingredients to mix, but nothing stood out to her as spectacular. And these beers needed to stand out in the sea of other incredible beers.

Maisie seemed to read her thoughts and gave a gentle smile. "Well, just know if you get totally stuck, we can keep with Foxy Diva this year and look into something like this next year. I have no doubt Ronnie would understand."

Yeah, he probably would, but Amelia wouldn't fail her sisters. Not when they'd done so much for the brewery. "I'll be fine," she said, both to her sisters and to herself. She shifted against her chair and she felt something tickling her back. She reached into her back pocket, discovering a piece of paper. "Oh, that sneaky man."

"What is it?" Maisie asked.

Amelia unfolded the check for ten thousand dollars, signed by Beckett, and showed it to her sisters. "Beckett wasn't too happy about my paying off Luka for the surgery."

Clara rolled her eyes. "There is no win-win here. Obviously, you weren't going to let him go to jail. You had no other choice if he was being too stubborn to pay Luka."

Amelia agreed with a nod.

Maisie asked, "Was it weird seeing Luka again?"

"Sort of," Amelia admitted. "But maybe it was better that I saw him right away. Kinda like ripping the Band-Aid off, and now I can walk away and not have to think about him anymore."

"You're probably right," Clara said gently. She made her way over to the table with three coffees on a tray and set them in front of each sister before taking a seat next to Maisie. "Beckett paid you back, then?"

"I told him I didn't want his money," Amelia said, hugging the warm mug with her hands. "This is my mess, not his."

"Apparently he disagrees with you," Maisie stated before taking a sip of her coffee.

"Yeah, apparently." Amelia snorted. "He snuck the check into my pocket at some point." Probably during that last kiss that nearly melted her into a puddle on the floor. She smiled at her sisters. "I'll just have to sneak it back in his."

"He's never going to give on this, Amelia," Clara countered, lifting her mug to her mouth. "It's a lot of money. That's from the inheritance Pops left you, and Beckett knows that."

Amelia watched Clara sip her coffee and didn't doubt her decision. "Beckett was just protecting me. He isn't paying for my mistake. I won't let it happen."

"I get that," Maisie said with a shrug.

A long pause followed as they drank their coffees before Clara addressed Amelia again, "I know you don't want to talk about it, but it's my job as your older sister to look out for you." She set her mug back down, leveling Amelia with a hard look. "I get wanting to have a rebound to forget about

Luka for good, but Beckett isn't a one-night stand. He can't ever be that for you."

Amelia's heart clenched in agreement. "Beckett isn't a rebound."

Maisie chimed in, "So, that kiss was nothing?"

"It was just a kiss. That's it," Amelia said in an instant. "A thank you for knocking Luka out."

Maisie barked a laugh. "That's some thank you."

Clara, though, wasn't laughing. She shook her head, and before taking another sip of her coffee, she said, "I hope you know what you're doing."

Amelia clicked mugs with Maisie. "Don't you worry about me. I know exactly what I'm doing."

## 6

**B**eckett sat in the middle of the paddock and didn't move for two hours. Autumn watched him closely the whole time, but she also hadn't turned away and continued eating. Had she done so, the training session would have gone differently. But he held her focus, her curiosity building about him. For the last two years that Beckett had seriously been training horses alongside Nash, he'd come to learn that patience was the only way to a horse's heart. Kindness mattered, of course. Trust also. But patience mattered the most, and through his journey with horses, his patience had grown stronger.

He stayed frozen when Autumn finally took a step toward him. When she stood a foot away, she lowered her head, getting a good look him. Another step. And one more after that. Until he let out a slow breath as she sniffed his hands resting on his knee. Sensing her stillness, he lifted his hand and ran it up her face. When she accepted that, he slowly rose. She took a step back. "Easy, sweetie." He offered his hand again, and when she leaned a little forward, he stroked her face again. Then he turned and walked away, letting that be how she remembered the first day. Her coming to him, not the other way around. The vet appointment was necessary to move ahead with her training, but the path forward with this particular mare was starting over and changing her relationship with humans.

When he left through the gate and relatched it, Autumn still watched him steadily. It was good he had her curiosity. He hoped that made their next steps easy ones. By the time he got behind the wheel of his truck, she returned to eating her hay. A good start.

The dust trailed his truck as he drove down the driveway. As much as he wanted to go home and have a quick shower and grab some grub, the very thought of Amelia saying to him, *"Come back after work, okay?"* had him skipping all that entirely. But first, he needed to make a couple stops.

He reached the first stop fifteen minutes later, finding his father on the porch, where he sat most evenings. A sad picture, really. Once his father's life had been filled with love and laughter, but those were things of the past now.

"Hey," Beckett said the moment he got out of his truck, slamming the door behind him.

"Hi, son," Jim replied, rocking in his chair.

Beckett took the seat next to him, staring out at the quiet road. "You look like you're in pretty good shape," he said, noting the rosy color of his cheeks.

Jim snorted. "You should have seen me a few hours ago."

Beckett was glad he hadn't. He kept his feet planted on the ground, not allowing the chair his mother used to sit in to rock. "Do you remember what happened?" he asked, glancing sidelong at his dad.

"Pieces of it..." Jim said before he trailed off. When he spoke again, emotion tightened his voice. "I'm sorry—"

"Don't," Beckett said, slowly shaking his head. "You don't need to apologize to me."

His father looked out toward the sunset. "Feels like I should."

At one point in Beckett's life, he would have wanted that apology and thought it meant something, but truth was, there was no fixing his father. He'd long ago accepted that. When Jim lost his wife, he died with her. There was no life in this house anymore. No life in his father anymore. Jim worked his construction job, then sat in front of his television. The only other thing he did was watch the sunset every night. Beckett knew why. His mother loved sunsets, and Jim did this to remember her.

"I can't stay," Beckett told his father, moving away from apologies and guilt, as his therapist once instructed him to do. He loved his father and saw him regularly, but Jim was existing, not living, yet Beckett wouldn't give up on him, hoping one day his father would break free from his grief. "I'm heading over to see Amelia tonight," he said, hoping that would brighten his father's mood. He'd always liked Amelia.

His father glanced sidelong. "She all right after all that happened to her?"

Beckett had caught his father up on the wedding that didn't happen, but he hadn't told his dad about the charges, not wanting to worry him. He nodded. "Yeah, she's all right."

"Good," Jim said, with a firm nod.

With nothing further to add, Beckett rose and cupped his father's shoulder, glad to see his father was in one piece. "Call if you need anything."

"You know I will."

His father wouldn't call. He never did, but Beckett understood why. Years of guilt and shame and loss and pain stole his father away. Beckett didn't hate him for the way he'd changed, but he no longer let his father's depression affect his life like it once had, because that pain had nearly drowned Beckett too.

Back on the road, he made one last quick stop at his house to make preparations for what he hoped was a good step in the right direction with Amelia, then he made his way to her.

Twenty minutes later, when he pulled up to her house, he found the barn's double doors still open, but all he discovered was an empty brewery. He headed up to the house and knocked on the door. Only silence greeted him. A glance over his shoulder revealed Amelia's car. Before he called her, he decided on a quick look in the backyard. There was one place Amelia loved more than her brewery. The mature Rocky Mountain Maple in her backyard. Which was exactly where he found her.

He couldn't figure out why she was surrounded by glass jars of herbs, spices and flowers. But he was mostly distracted by the fact that she had changed in a yellow sundress. Christ, she looked pretty. "Planning to bake today?"

She glanced up and gave him a half-smile. "Trying to find inspiration."

"In there?" he asked, gesturing to the jars.

"Everything here is what goes into the beer," she explained, the evening sunlight hitting her hair just right to make the ginger color shimmer. "Ronnie asked me to come up with six samples for him."

"Come up with anything yet?" Beckett said, dropping down onto the grass next to her.

"No," she said, glaring at the glass jars. "Maybe I'm just stuck because I know I have so much work ahead of me, but everything I'm coming up with is just boring or has been done before."

He wondered how he'd find Amelia this evening. If she'd be full of regret, but she only seemed focused on her work. He noted the tension creasing her eyes. "Anything I can help with?"

She set her clever eyes on him. "Got any ideas how to make my mind clear?"

He couldn't help himself. He grinned devilishly. "I've got a few."

Her mouth twitched. "Serious ideas for a new beer that will knock peoples socks off?"

He winked. "Anything with a high alcohol count usually does the trick."

She laughed softly. The tension on her face melting away. "If it were only that easy."

Christ, he loved when she smiled that like. He'd wondered if she knew she stopped smiling like that when she was with the prick.

"Ronnie's got one distribution spot open to market the hell out of a brewery with quarterly beers, and three breweries are fighting for the spot." She ran her hands over her face and sighed heavily. "There's just so much to do. I should have cleaned out the beer tanks today, but my entire day got eaten up with visits and then I started thinking about these samples I need to do for Ronnie and got stuck on that." She dropped her hands, sighing again. "It's just a lot, you know?"

"You've got this, Am. Give yourself time. You only just got back today."

"You're right," she finally said. "All I'm doing is beating myself up. Nothing is going to come from this tonight." She began fastening the lids onto the jars.

Beckett helped her until he closed the last lid. "If you've got some time, can I take you somewhere?"

She looked up at him through her thick lashes. "I've got to get started on cleaning my tanks out."

He gestured toward the sunset. "There's no way you'll get through it tonight. Today was a busy, long day. Start fresh tomorrow."

She studied the sunset and then sighed again. "Okay, yeah, it won't kill me to start tomorrow."

"No, it won't." He smiled, offering his hand. She accepted his help up as she got to her feet, and he fought the urge to tug her close and keep her there.

Instead, he let her go and she wiped her hands on her dress. "Where do you want to go?"

He motioned to the front of the house. "Come with me and you'll see."

Intrigue sparkled in her eyes as she followed him. The same excitement danced on her face as he opened the passenger side door of his truck. Her expression only shifted when they drove into his backyard and the brightest smile filled her face.

"You're kidding?" she asked.

His breath caught at that smile. The beauty in it. The sweetness. "Not kidding. You used to love this. I thought you might like to do it again." He placed a hand low on the small of her back and guided her forward toward the blanket set out in the field, with the projector facing the barn. Backyard movie nights were their thing back in high school.

"I still love this," she said with a tender smile. "I just haven't done it in a really long time." When they reached the blanket, she noted the dill pickle chips, Coke, and black licorice on the blanket before she grinned up at him. "You remembered my favorite treats?"

He nodded with a laugh. "It was all you ate back then, how could I possibly forget?" He motioned for her to sit. "Go. I'll get the movie on." The sun had nearly set now as he sensed her taking a seat and couldn't fight his smile, anticipating her reaction. The second he hit play, he glanced back and saw her eyes widen and her smile beam when she saw he put on *The Breakfast Club*.

Her sparkling gaze met his. "You're pulling out all the stops tonight. My favorite movie too?"

He wondered, *when was the last time anyone did something just for her?* By her surprise it seemed like a long time. "I know this movie word for word," he told her, returning to her side. He'd never tell her that he watched this movie more than he'd ever admit aloud because it reminded him of her. As the movie began, he opened the chips and dumped them into the bowl before he opened the licorice bag.

Amelia sat looking at the movie, but every so often looked at the chips.

Beckett laughed. "I've seen you inhale chips and licorice in ten minutes flat. What are you waiting for? They're not going to bite you." He didn't like the way she hesitated, telling him that bastard likely commented on how she ate food she loved quickly. He picked up the bowl and handed to her, but not before grabbing a huge handful and shoving it in his mouth. "I'm going to eat them all if you don't," he said with a full mouth.

She laughed softly and began eating.

Feeling like he could stay right here a lifetime and never want to leave, he leaned back on one arm and grabbed some licorice, devouring it as the movie continued. They laughed at the same parts as they had back in high school. She quoted lines, and he followed, and it began to feel like no time had passed between them at all.

Beckett reached for another licorice when something else hit his mouth instead. He caught up to Amelia's kiss in an instant, but let her lead the way, following her open-mouthed kiss but never taking over to deepen it.

Many *many* minutes later when she pulled away, she asked, "Is it all right that I do that?"

He chuckled. "Yeah, Am, it's all right." He stared into her pretty eyes and gave her a smile, thinking of how he left her earlier and figuring it was a conversation they couldn't ignore. "I take it, since I'm not dead, everything went well with your sisters after I left this morning."

Amelia shrugged. "Maisie was Maisie about it all. And Clara was Clara, worried and overprotective."

"I'm sure we shocked them."

Her sensual laughter made his cock twitch. "Just a little." Then her laughter fell, expression tightened. "I know I'm in this really weird place in my life right now. The last thing I should be doing is letting anything like this happen, but I don't regret kissing you."

Best thing he'd ever heard. "Good. Neither do I."

She nibbled her lip, drawing his full attention to her pouty mouth. "I just don't want to hurt you, and a lot has happened. I can't really even explain why I grabbed you and kissed you, other than to say it felt right to do that."

"I'm glad you did it this morning," he said with a grin. "And just now too."

Her eyes crinkled at the corners with her smile. "Clara's really worried my head is not on straight, and to be honest, it probably isn't. I just don't want that to—"

He pressed a finger against her lip, stopping that conversation in its tracks. He wasn't in a rush. He'd waited years to have her looking at him like she was looking at him now. As long as she was kissing him and not someone else, he could wait until she was ready for something serious. Instead of hitting her with all that truth she probably wasn't ready for, he said, "Let me worry about me."

She drew in a visibly trembling breath, a pinkish hue creeping over her cheeks that had nothing to do with shyness. "Okay."

Seeing the resolve on her face, he gathered her in his

arms then, pulling her underneath him, intending to show her just how okay he was with all this. How he'd give to her, not taking anything back, only to have *her*. "I want to kiss you."

Her cheeks pinkened. "I want you to kiss me too."

He couldn't fight his grin before he slanted his mouth across hers again, dragging his hand up her thigh, bringing her dress higher up her thigh. He broke the kiss to gaze upon her, and her chest rose and fell rapidly. His rough breathing matched hers. "You've changed, do you know that?" he asked, feeling her tremble beneath his touch.

"How have I changed?" she rasped when he slid a hand across her thigh.

"You're all woman now," he told her, hearing the huskiness in his voice. She'd been eighteen when she'd offered her virginity to him. She'd been nineteen the last time his hands were on her. Her body was rounder now, hips slightly larger. He slid his hand between her and the blanket, cupping her ass. Then he dropped his head into her neck. She angled to the side, giving him access, and he slowly licked and nibbled his way up to her ear. "You feel so fucking good, Am."

Her moan was her reply.

Intending to give her more, he caught her mouth, and she met his intensity at every turn. She followed his open-mouthed kiss, dancing her tongue alongside his, and he couldn't get enough.

When he leaned away, her gaze did a thorough once-over of him from head-to-toe, causing his cock to jump when she stared at him with such hunger. "You've changed too." She reached out and ran a hand over his chest, his biceps and forearms, stopping once we reached his shoulders. "You're so strong."

*Strong enough to carry all your burdens.* But he kept silent, embracing the tight hold she had on him. The way she touched him so intimately, so passionately, had him sealing his mouth across hers again. Her heady moans filled his ears, and for the first time in a very long time, he felt like he was finally getting something right.

## 7

The next morning, Amelia stared down at the crumbs on her small plate from her cheese croissant, waiting and wondering if regret would suddenly surface after what happened with Beckett last night. It never came. Something else didn't come either – guilt. Shouldn't there be some of that? Sure, Luka left her at the altar and embarrassed her in front of everyone, but she'd loved him and had planned a life with him. Why wasn't she feeling horrible for making out with Beckett so soon after her breakup? And why was Beckett on her mind all the time? Thoughts of his sweet tongue and delicious pleasure kept her thinking of him all morning. His throaty voice stuck in her ear, raising goosebumps along the skin he'd touched. The way he commanded her body like he owned her made her shiver.

She didn't know this Beckett. She knew the young, wild Beckett who took her virginity. Then she knew a more distant side of Beckett after his mother and grandfather died. A Beckett who gave up on his dreams of the rodeo and had taken a giant step back from her. The man that touched her yesterday didn't feel like the one who told her there was distance between them and he couldn't give her what she wanted. Hell no, he was strong and solid, every spectacular inch of him. But what stayed on her mind most was his sweet gesture with the movie. That was a Beckett she did know. One who thought of her instead of himself, remembered the little things, and knew her more than anyone else. She'd forgotten that about him. How much he paid attention, and how he went out of his way to make her happy. She really missed that. Luka didn't even know dill pickle was her favorite chip flavor. Maybe Luka hadn't known her that well at all.

Deciding to get her day going and not let anything interrupt her getting her brewery back in order, she set to cleaning up. As she finished washing her plate, she heard the rumble of a truck coming up her driveway, followed by a few more. She quickly set the plate in the drying rack, then dried her hands on the towel resting over the stove's handle. By the time she opened the front door, two more trucks were coming up the driveway. Her heart sank in her throat, hoping Penelope hadn't forgotten to cancel any of the brewery tours.

The worry was short lived as she spotted Beckett's truck leading the group, and then noticed two of the other trucks had BLACKSHAW HORSE TRAINING written on them.

"What's going on?" she asked the moment Beckett exited his truck.

"Help."

She blinked, processed, but still felt lost. "Sorry, help with what exactly?"

He reached her at her porch steps, giving her a bright smile that she'd like to think she had a hand in. "Yesterday you said that you needed to get your tanks cleaned up." He gestured back with a flick of his chin at the three cowboys

71

behind him. "Nash didn't mind us coming here to help you get settled."

Her heart overflowed with emotions, and she placed a hand on her chest to keep her heart from beating right out of her chest. "I can't accept help."

Beckett's brows knitted. "Why not?"

"Because it's just too much. You guys have your own stuff going on. Seriously, thank you, but this is way too much."

Beckett watched her closely for a long moment before he headed up the two steps to stand directly in front of her, heating up the air with him. Her heart raced for a whole different reason now, as he said, "This isn't the time to feel bad. You need the help. It's here. Take it."

She stared into the warm comfort in his gaze, realizing she truly did need the help. "You're really sure Nash okayed this?"

Beckett gave a firm nod. "Of course, Amelia, we've got your back."

Without thought, she threw her arms around his neck, hugging him tight, and he enveloped her in his strong arms. "Thank you for this, Beckett. It's truly above and beyond."

He dropped his head into her neck, and she swore she heard his long inhale before he said, "No thanks required." He leaned away but didn't release her, hitting her with that sparkling grin again. "The boys love your beer, so it only benefits them to get the spoiled beer out and good beer back in"

She became lost in the strength in his eyes. Truth was, she never allowed herself to look too hard at Beckett, not fully trusting her heart while she was with Luka. She certainly saw all of him now, and she really liked the man he'd become, and how much he helped her whenever he could.

"I see this is becoming a habit."

Amelia jerked away at hearing Clara's voice, though

Beckett's hands stayed firmly on her hips. A flurry of reasons popped into her mind to explain their embrace, but she gave up and just ignored Clara's dig. "Beckett brought some of the guys over to help clean out the tanks."

"Yes, I heard," she said, giving Beckett an inquisitive look.

Amelia felt the tension thicken in the air and decided to get Clara and Beckett as far away from each other as possible. "Hey guys," she called to the group of cowboys. They all turned her way. One of the men she knew from high school. "I really appreciate you helping out today. You've got no idea how much this will help get me back on track. Lunch and beers are on us."

Hooting and hollering followed as Mason, her six-year-old nephew, who was turning seven in a few short months, ran for Amelia. Beckett moved out of the way right as Mason flew at her. She caught him in her arms, giving him a big hug. "I've missed you so much, buddy."

"Me too, Aunty Amelia."

She leaned away. "Shouldn't you be at school?"

"I have a day off so teachers can do paperwork and stuff." He grinned before taking off toward the cowboys, heading into the brewery.

Beckett chuckled. "I take it that means it's time to work." He glanced between Amelia and Clara, winked and flicked his cowboy hat. "See ya in there."

Amelia swallowed the heat simmering in her core and nodded. "I'll be along in one second."

His panty-melting grin was the last thing she saw before he walked away. As soon as he was out of earshot, she whirled around to Clara. "You are being seriously rude. What the hell is wrong with you?"

Clara crossed her arms, frowning. "Protective, not rude."

"No, it's rude, trust me," Amelia shot back. She pointed to the brewery. "Beckett brought these guys here to help me after I told him yesterday that I had a lot to do, and I was finding it overwhelming."

Clara's expression pinched. "You're not thinking clearly, Amelia, and that makes me very worried."

Not this again. Amelia threw up her arms. "I already told you that you don't need to worry about me. I'm fine. Leave it alone."

Clara's nostrils flared. "How can you be? Honestly, two weeks ago you were supposed to marry another man. Now you're heating things up again with the guy that you once said was your one and only. How is any of that fine, Amelia?"

Okay, so it was confusing. "Seriously, *nothing* is happening." Well, a few things were happening, but it was none of her sister's business.

Clara inhaled a deep breath before the deepest glare Amelia had ever seen in her life crossed her sister's face. "He's not only your friend—you are aware of this, right? I care very deeply about Beckett too. And *this*... Amelia, what you are doing to him is cruel. He has never stopped loving you. *Never.* He's been patiently waiting to see if he ever had another chance with you. If you don't realize that, you're stupid."

Amelia glared now. "Harsh."

"I'm not sugarcoating this for anyone," Clara said, coldly, matter-of-factly. "I stood by and watched you fall in love with a total shithead, and I said nothing. But both you and Beckett need to wake up and see that this is a dangerous game you're playing." Her sister leaned in and narrowed her eyes, pointing a finger in Amelia's face. "As much as I don't want him to hurt you, I don't want you to hurt him."

"I have no plans to hurt him," Amelia said in all seriousness.

Clara didn't back down. Her eyes narrowed further into slits. "Is your head clear enough to even make that decision?"

*Yes,* nearly escaped her mouth, but the word couldn't find its way through her lips. She took a deep breath and considered. Clara rubbed a lot of people wrong. Not Amelia. She appreciated that Clara didn't wear a mask or hold back. "Fine, I've heard you, and I'll take what you've said into consideration," was Amelia's carefully worded reply.

"Good," Clara said, softer this time. "That's all I ask. Think this through and don't blindly walk around pretending that what you two are doing is not a huge deal." She finally huffed and gave Amelia a quick kiss on the cheek. "Now let's go save those cowboys from Mason."

Amelia laughed softly, even though it felt a little forced. She strode next to Clara as they approached the brewery, absorbing the conversation. She couldn't deny she wasn't thinking things through completely, but she'd done that with Luka and that only got her dumped at the altar. Beckett was a grown man. He seemed happy, why couldn't Clara get on board with that too? The cowboys were talking and laughing, and considering no one was covering their noses, she thought that was a good sign.

"All right, boss," Beckett said when she stepped into the brewery. He leaned against the tank, looking like a woman's dream come true, with Mason hanging off his arm. "Put us to work."

She smiled at how much Mason always seemed to love being around Beckett before she looked at her helpers for the day. "I hope you all don't mind getting dirty."

Laughter echoed through the brewery.

Smirking to herself, considering they had no idea what they were in for, she climbed the ladder and opened the tank. The scent of rancid grain quickly infused the air. Each and every one of them covered their noses. One even gagged. "Anyone want to back out now?" she asked.

They all glanced at Beckett.

He glared.

"Where do we start?" one of the cowboys called.

§⚶

BECKETT LOADED the last of the plates in the dishwasher before he caught Amelia laughing at something Chevy, one of the young stable hands at the ranch, had said. He wondered if she knew that she was laughing easier since she'd come home. He hadn't seen her laugh like this in a very long time. If he was being honest, he hadn't seen this sweet laughter from her since before the accident, and Beckett took blame in that.

Cleaning the tanks and disposing of the spoiled grain had taken longer than expected. Amelia had ordered pizza for lunch, but Clara and Amelia had made a home-cooked meal when cleaning the brewery took up until dinnertime, but they'd managed to get it done. All in all, the day was success-ful, and Beckett was glad she could get ahead of the game. The sun was beginning to set, bathing the gorgeous sky in pink and purple hues, and Beckett took a deep breath. Things had been bad for a very long time, and then even when they were no longer bad, they were lonely. Sure, Beckett took women to his bed to fill the void of Amelia's absence, but they never lasted, because he gave nothing of himself. Now, as he looked upon Amelia laughing, he wondered if things were about to take a turn for the better.

"What exactly are you doing here, Beckett?"

He sighed at Clara's sharp voice. Christ, she was relent-less. He closed the dishwasher and then glanced back, meeting her hard gaze. He had it in him to remind her *again* that whatever was going between him and Amelia didn't include Clara's input, but he saw the raw concern on Clara's face. "Taking care of her."

Unforgiving eyes searched his. "Is that it, then? You're looking out for her?"

"That's it," he told her, not feeling the need to explain that, if Amelia would give him her heart, he'd take it and protect it forever.

"What about you?" Clara asked, with a rare gentle voice. "Who's looking out for you in all this? Can you really handle a fling with Amelia, since it's pretty clear that a serious relationship is the last thing on her mind?"

Her words hit him like a brick to the chest. It hadn't occurred to him that Clara would worry for his wellbeing. She shocked him into silence for a few seconds. "I'm looking out for myself," he eventually answered, "but thank you for your concern."

Everything typically hard on Clara softened as she took him by the arms, holding them tightly as she looked into his eyes. "I have waited for this reunion for a long time. Please, *please*, take this slow and easy so that it works out and you both come out of this happy."

Leaving him utterly speechless now, she exited the back door and made her way back to Sullivan and Mason. He processed what she'd told him. He had no idea that she wanted them to reunite. Or what he should do with that information.

Damn. He always thought Clara would want better for Amelia. He screwed up once before, and he'd never amounted to much since then— never competed professionally like he had planned or become wealthy. Though he supposed he should have realized that between Luka and him, Beckett was definitely a better match in every way that mattered.

When Beckett followed Amelia outside, Clara and Sullivan were saying their goodbyes with Mason giving Amelia a big squeeze.

"Bye, buddy," Beckett said to him as Mason approached. He gave him a high five. "Kick butt at your game this weekend."

Mason did a ninja move and yelled incoherent words before running toward the front of the house.

Clara shook her head at her retreating son. "I swear sometimes he's living in a world entirely his own."

"Not a bad thing," Beckett said with a smile.

"No, it's not," Clara replied, then shocking him again, she hugged him. "Thanks again for your help today. We really appreciate it and won't forget it anytime soon."

"I'm glad to help," he said, hugging her back.

He remained in a state of shock until Sullivan grinned at him, cupping his shoulder. "Let's get a beer and wings before I head back to Boston."

"Just let me know when," Beckett said.

"Done," Sullivan said.

By the time Sullivan left the backyard, Nash's cowboys started to leave too. They laughed as they made their way to their trucks, their bellies full from the dinner Amelia and Clara cooked for them, as well as the couple beers as a thank you. Of course, Amelia sent them all home with a case of Foxy Diva too.

"Stay for a fire?"

Beckett turned around, finding Amelia smiling behind him. "Sure thing," he said. He grabbed another beer from the cooler, his last one for the evening. After a long sip, he set his bottle on the bench, then grabbed the axe, cutting up some wood while Amelia gathered the kindling and started the fire.

"I heard about your dad," she said, as the kindling began to burn.

"Not much of a surprise. I'm sure the whole town is

talking about it." Beckett knelt next to her and placed three logs in a teepee formation around the kindling.

Her gaze met his, understanding there. "Days connected to your mom always seem so hard on him."

It surprised him Amelia remembered his mother's birthday. "They are," he agreed, moving to the Adirondack chair and stretching out his legs as smoke bellowed from the logs. "Luckily he didn't cause too much trouble. Just passed out in the park."

"That's good," she said, taking the seat next to him. "He never could find his way home, huh?"

Beckett took a long sip of his beer before placing it on the armrest. "Nope, never could." Sometimes he wondered what went through his dad's head, but he didn't like being in that space long. He'd lost Amelia, he knew what that felt like, but he was only looking toward the future now.

"Besides that," said Amelia, drawing his attention back to her. "How's your dad doing?"

Beckett shrugged. "He's existing."

"What do you mean by that?"

"He's not really living," Beckett explained as the fire crackled, the logs finally catching. "All he does is wake up, work and then watch television."

Amelia slowly shook her head, obvious disappoint on her expression. "The whole thing is still so sad. So much loss."

Beckett nodded agreement, looking into the blazing fire. "It's sad, yes, but it's also a battle you can't win." He tried for years to get his father help with his all-consuming grief, but when Beckett realized he'd lost everything that mattered, that his father wanted to stay under that dark cloud of despair, he had to stop trying to help his father and accept that Jim didn't want to be saved.

"Do you ever wonder what life would have been like if the accident didn't happen?"

"Yeah," Beckett said, a lump rising in this throat. "I used to think about that a lot. I suspect I'd be a pro in the rodeo, and you'd be—"

She gave a soft smile, the words hanging between them —*my wife.*

Beckett shifted in his chair, refusing to let his mind go there. "But life isn't for our choosing. Things happen, and you just have to roll with it."

"I guess you do," she agreed, then her expression shifted, becoming a little more distant.

Beckett knew why. She was thinking of all her life choices and where they got her, but the blame for her life going wrong all landed in Beckett's lap. Had he not lost his way after the accident, he would have proposed to her before she left for college and drove up to see her whenever he could. They would have made it work. But he had lost his way, and shut Amelia out of his life. That would never happen again.

To get her out of her head, he tapped her arm with his. "Getting lost in there?" he asked.

She glanced his way and smiled. "A little." Her expression shifted then, and Beckett felt the heat roll through him in an instant. "But I'm also thinking of something else we could do that's much more fun than talking about all the heavy stuff." She rose and climbed onto his lap, and he wrapped his arms around her back as she thrust her hands into his hair. "Don't you?"

"Mm hmm," he told her.

She licked her lips and he had to use all his strength not to claim that mouth. "Want to come inside?"

Damn did he want to. The heat building in his groin agreed. But Clara's talk rattled him. He couldn't shake what she said: *Please, please, take this slow and easy so that it works out and you both come out of this happy.* The last thing he wanted to do was take a wrong step. Once everything got away from him and he'd lost Amelia, his dreams of becoming a professional calf roper, and his family in one fell swoop. He'd never let anything get away from him again. His steps needed to stay focused and his mind had to remain clear. "Actually, I'm beat. It's been a long day. Is it all right if I take a raincheck?"

Obvious disappointment flashed across her expression. "Sure, of course."

He kissed the top of her forehead and then rose, setting her back to her feet. "I'll see you tomorrow?"

She nodded. "I'd like that."

"Me, too." Unable to help himself, as she looked up at him with those cute eyes, he took her chin and slanted his mouth across hers. She fell into his kiss, pressing her lush body against him, offering him whatever he wanted. And it was the purest form of hell when he broke the kiss and walked away.

## 8

Whenthe alarm went off the following morning, Amelia groaned her displeasure. She snatched up her cellphone off her nightstand and turned the alarm off, feeling like she'd hardly slept at all. Last night all she'd done was toss and turn, a thousand thoughts spinning on her mind. The biggest, most important one: why did Beckett not jump at the chance to sleep with her? She'd known he'd always been sweet, but who was this patient man who didn't think of sex first? Beckett was pure passion, or at least he had been when she'd first met him in high school, when she was a freshman and he was a senior. He'd always had his eyes set on the rodeo, never planning on going to college. He knew his path and what he wanted out of life, *her* included, and she'd fallen madly in love with that passion. But in Amelia's final month of high school, the accident took his mother and grandfather's life, and Beckett's world shattered. She'd stayed with him until weeks before she left for college, fighting for their relationship. But she'd failed to reach him again. He'd told her to go and move on, and she had. Beckett wasn't pushing her away anymore, but he wasn't rushing things either. He was the same passionate, sweet guy she once knew, but he wasn't letting things go any further. She couldn't figure out what game he was playing or if he was playing a game at all.

Figuring she was just going to drive herself crazy by thinking this over, she set to showering and getting ready for her day. Down in the kitchen twenty minutes later, she watched the coffee maker brew and yawned when her front door opened.

"Amelia?" Penelope called.

"In here," Amelia answered, pouring herself a cup of coffee and adding sugar and cream before stirring it. She caught the incredible scent of baked apples and smiled before Penelope walked through the doorway. "You brought my favorite?" she asked.

Penelope offered the box with a smile. "It's my bribe for you to tell me everything going on with you and Beckett."

Amelia laughed, happily accepting the box. "It's a good bribe." She set the box down on the counter and opened the lid, her mouth instantly watering. The apple fritters from the bakery downtown were the best, and Amelia took a bite before she added, "Honestly, there is not much to tell, but thanks for breakfast."

Penelope took another one of the to-go mugs out of the cupboard and made herself a coffee before giving Amelia a once-over. "If there's nothing much to tell, then why do you look so perturbed?"

Amelia lifted her brows. "I look perturbed?"

"Okay, weird word, I know," Penelope said, and then gave a slight shrug. "But that's how you look. Like, bothered in a way I've never seen you bothered before."

Amelia snatched up her to-go mug with her free hand. "Come on, I need to get some beer brewing and I'll explain."

Penelope quickly followed Amelia out of the house,

devouring her apple fritter on the way. When Amelia entered the brewery, she inhaled the clean scent and smiled. This she could work with. Brewing Foxy Diva was second nature now. Their beloved brew had come from their pops' home-made brew that Amelia had altered a little after he passed. Amelia never would have told him during his life his beer was too bitter and too heavy, but all the Indian pale ale needed was a little love and it became a beer Amelia found pride in.

"All right, stop stalling and spill it," Penelope said.

"First, follow me." Amelia headed over to the milling station where a sanitized bucket sat beneath the mill. She grabbed a heavy bag of barley, she cut the top and using a grain scoop, she filled the mill to the top. She turned on the motorized mill, then stepped back closer to Penelope as the mill ground up the grain to expose the starches insides so the water could extract sugars and other unwanted ingredients. "I guess I am little perturbed. So, things with Beckett... well, they're heating up."

Penelope cocked her head. "Is that a bad thing?"

Amelia tried to gather up the thoughts running through her head, and she failed miserably. "It's confusing, because is this wrong?"

Penelope took a seat on one of the turned over buckets. "Seeing him, you mean?"

"Yeah," Amelia said, nibbling her lip as she added some more barley into the mill to crush the grain. "First of all, is it healthy for me to get involved with anyone so soon after Luka?"

Penelope frowned. "He did leave you at the altar. I'm not so sure you need to feel bad for anything, especially if that *something* is making you happy."

Amelia considered that. "I guess, but should I go back to

Beckett, to the past? Or am I just setting myself up for more heartbreak here?"

Penelope paused and gave a knowing look. "No matter who you date you always set yourself up for heartbreak." Her expression softened. "But sometimes it works out if you take a leap of faith."

Amelia exhaled a slowly breath. "But is it too soon to take that leap? We've got a complicated history. A past where there was a lot of love, but we grew apart. He knew that. I knew that. Our lives went in two different directions."

"Okay, I get that," Penelope said. "But you've certainly found your way back to each other."

Amelia hit the stop on the mill and switched out the bucket beneath for an empty one. While she put on the lid on the full bucket, she added, "I think that might be the problem."

"Because…?" Penelope drawled.

Amelia stopped dancing around what was going on in her heart. She turned to Penelope, and in the warm friendship she had with her cousin, she laid it all on the line. "Because last night, Beckett didn't take a step forward with me. He took a step back, and I'm bothered. Clara kept warning me that it couldn't be a casual thing with Beckett, which I knew, but honestly, he was just making me feel good and happy and I liked that. I thought it could be casual. So why am I torn up that he didn't want to come to my bed last night? We kissed and stuff, but this isn't kissing and stuff feelings, this is *more.* And I just can't help but wonder if I'm making a big mistake here. I mean, I was just left at the altar, about to marry someone else. Shouldn't I be more broken up about that?"

Awareness filled Penelope's eyes. "No, because that asshat made a mess of your heart. You're allowed to move on from Luka the very next day if Beckett makes you happy."

A headache loomed, and Amelia rubbed at her temple.

"So, is that what it is? You feel like it's too soon?"

Amelia sighed, adding more barley to the mill before continuing. "It feels like it's too soon for anything serious. But I also feel rejected and hurt that he turned me down last night, and I'm not sure I have the right to feel that way."

"I see," Penelope said. "That is confusing."

"Exactly," Amelia agreed with a nod. The mill suddenly stopped, and Amelia sighed once more, pushing the thoughts from her mind. Clara was right – she didn't have a clear head, and she needed to get that before she saw Beckett again. The last thing she wanted to do was hurt him. "I really need to get a couple batches of Foxy Diva going. What are your plans for today?"

"I'll be in the office arranging tours for next weekend now that you're back." Penelope opened her arms, and Amelia walked into them as her cousin offered, "Maybe all you and Beckett need is to have a really good talk about what he wants out of this. Maybe he's just holding back because he doesn't want to rush you, considering what happened with Luka." She hesitated, then gave Amelia a sweet smile. "Beckett has been single for a long time. He punched Luka square in the face when he broke your heart. It doesn't take a rocket scientist to see why he did that."

"Maybe," Amelia said. "Thanks for the talk." She stepped out of Penelope's arms. "Love you."

"Love you back." Penelope blew her a kiss before heading toward the office.

With Penelope gone, Amelia focused on her work, grabbing the full buckets and headed over to the mash tun, where the crushed malt gets mixed with very hot water, creating enzymes that convert the starches in the malt into sugars and dextrins that eventually becomes the body of the beer. She fell into the rhythm of brewing the beer she loved. Once the mash was complete, the liquid now in the boil kettle to boil for the next ninety minutes, she cleaned the mash tun, putting the spent grain in a large tub that the Blackshaw Cattle Ranch would pick up to use as livestock feed. And by the time the second batch of Foxy Diva passed through the heat exchanger to cool before fermentation, she could finally breathe again, knowing she had the brewery back in order.

She'd spent a few hours coming up with sample ideas, only to realize in the end the ingredients wouldn't give her anything she hadn't seen before. Frustrated, and beating her head against the wall to come up with something new and fresh, she finally stepped out a couple hours before dinner, wiping the sweat off her forehead. A quick look next to the brewery and she realized that Penelope had left at some point, but everyone knew not to interrupt Amelia when she was brewing. She quickly took stock of her emotions, and realized she still felt *off* about Beckett.

Deciding she couldn't wait any longer to get this resolved, she hopped in her car and drove over to Beckett's work, knowing if he hadn't called yet, he was likely training. As soon she drove up the driveway, she spotted him working a gorgeous strawberry roan horse in the sand ring. Not wanting to disturb him, she pulled off to the side of the driveway and got out, taking a seat on the hood of car and watching him.

One thing she had loved about Beckett back in the day was the respect and love he had for horses. Before the tragic accident, he'd had his beloved horse, Smokey, that he'd trained from a colt. That horse would have taken him all the way to the top. Together, they'd climbed up the calf roping rankings so fast, and his grandfather always looked on with pride. But everything changed after the accident. Beckett changed. Gone were his hopes and dreams, and he'd lost all his ambition to continue with the rodeo. And, in turn, he'd lost his way… and her too, giving up on their relationship and ending it without giving her a chance to save it.

And she'd tried to save it. She tried so damn hard. But Amelia had seen her once beautiful life with Beckett vanish, her happiness disappear, and no matter that it ripped her heart out to leave Beckett, she had to continue with her life. Only she couldn't have imagined this was where she'd end up.

Standing in the center of the ring, Beckett clucked his tongue and hit the rope he held against his leg, sending the horse cantering around the sand ring. He stepped a little closer, lifting up the rope, the horse skidded to a halt, spun, and then after Beckett tapped his leg again, the horse cantered off. Watching his connection to horses felt so familiar, so good.

He clucked his tongue again and the horse moved faster, and Beckett began working the rope over his head. Every move precise. Each circle of his wrist exact. And at the exact right moment, he threw the rope, expertly sliding it over the horse's head with ease. He pulled the horse tight and called, "Whoa."

The mare stopped and turned directly to him. Amelia didn't know much about horses, but Beckett had always told her that when he had the horse's eye contact and curiosity, he had everything.

For a reason she didn't quite know, she needed to get closer, just to get a peek of that smile on his face. A smile so familiar, and one she hadn't seen in so long. When she closed in and caught the full force of it, her breath hitched as everything in her finally settled, like the sand in the ring returning back to the hard ground. Beckett looked at peace, and she felt right at home.

SOME COWBOYS MISSED the beauty of truly connecting with a horse, earning that horse's trust, and developing a relationship. But Beckett always took the time to make that connection as a teenager, training horses with his grandfather. And he took the time now, reveling in watching Autumn learn to trust him. Earlier today when he roped Autumn, she'd bolted, running in fear. Now she turned to face him, looking to him for guidance. A step in the right direction. He approached and she lowered her head as he stroked her face. "You might have a lot of fire, sweetheart, but you sure as hell got a lot of heart." She nudged him away and he laughed, slowly taking the rope over her head.

As he turned to give her a much-needed break before he ponied her out for a ride to finish off their day, he caught the most unexpected surprise leaning against the fence. "My day just got better," he told Amelia, approaching her.

She smiled, and the closer he got, the more he locked into the warmth in Amelia's eyes, the softness there. She had not looked at him like this in... he couldn't remember the last time.

"What's got you smiling?" he asked, settling at the fence between them.

She stepped onto the bottom fence, resting her arms on top. "It's been so long since I've seen you rope. You had the biggest smile on your face. Did you know that?"

He didn't realize he had been smiling. "No, did I?"

"The biggest I've seen on your face in a very long time," she said, her eyes smiling at him. "You're so in your element. Do you miss it?"

"I never let myself miss it," he told her, speaking a truth he'd never say aloud before. "When I decided to walk away from competing, I made peace with that."

Her eyes narrowed in thought like she was searching for

something. She finally asked, "Did you decide to walk away or was that chosen for you?"

He hesitated. "Fair point." He glanced back to Autumn, who was eating the grass around the ring, realizing it wasn't exactly a choice. To Amelia, he explained, "The accident changed things. It took away things. Things I couldn't get back."

She nibbled her lip, then offered, "Maybe it didn't take away as much as you think. It sure looks like you still have a love for horsemanship, and clearly you're still at the top of your game with roping."

He was at his best, though he didn't feel the need to confirm it. He'd never stopped training, never stopped roping whenever he got the chance. But he'd given up that dream a long time ago. "I can't even imagine getting back into the rodeo. The traveling for competitions..."

Her smile brightened. "The traveling is the fun part. Remember all the places we went?"

"Yeah." It occurred to him then that he'd done his best not to think about those memories too much. "We got to see some great places."

She glanced at the horse, and Beckett took the time to admire the short jean shorts she wore and the navy-blue tank top that hugged her body in all the right ways. "Do you ever talk to any of your old friends from the rodeo?" she asked, drawing his attention back to her face.

The color in her cheeks told him she'd noticed his attention. He shook his head. "Tried to keep in touch, but it's like two different lives in the rodeo and out of it."

"That's too bad," she said. "You had some good buddies in there."

He nodded his response, not denying that fact. But what was done was done, and that life belonged to his past, not his future. To change the subject, he asked, "What brings you by?"

"Oh," she said, and then hesitated, nibbling that lip again. "I hit wall after wall trying to come up with new samples. Nothing worked. Everything sucked. So, instead of beating myself up, I wondered if you felt like hanging out."

All that nibbling on her lip had him feeling like hanging in bed with her, but as he looked at the horse, he wasn't ready to end his workday yet. "I need to get a short ride out and pony her." An idea suddenly presented itself, and the thought warmed him. They always rode together back in the day, just the two of them. They'd spend hours out riding in the meadows and rolling in the grass whenever they could get their hands on each other. "Would you like to join us?"

Her eyes widened. "Go on a ride?" At his nod, she added, "Would Nash mind that?"

"Not at all," Beckett told her. "We always need the lazy horses out for a ride and none of the cowboys like taking them out. You can ride Larry."

She took a step backward as Beckett climbed the fence. "Who's Larry?" she asked.

He hit the ground. "A fat, old horse that Nash bought Megan to ride when she was pregnant. Trust me when I tell you that he's safe, won't take a step out of place, and he most definitely needs the exercise."

She laughed. "Okay, then yes, I'd love to go for a ride. It's been so long."

"How long?" he asked.

Her cheeks filled with beautiful color. "I only ever rode with you."

Damn, he liked that something belonged just to them. "Well, then, let's grab the tack and the horses and get out there."

His chest swelled with happiness as she stepped into stride with him toward the barn. He led her down the aisle, with box stalls on either side. The only time horses came inside the barn was if they were injured or needed stall training. Nash believed in natural horsemanship with horses living outside as much as possible, and Beckett agreed with that method too.

She took a look around. "Is it always so quiet here?"

"No," Beckett said, dryly. Most days there was a flurry of activity at the farm. "The team is moving the mares to another pasture to let the grass grow. It's an all-day job."

"Cool," she said. A pause. Then her voice turned bubbly, "Oh, my goodness, how sweet is this?"

Beckett looked at what caught her attention. He smiled, fully understanding the sweetness in her voice. "It's actually a bit of a sad story that has a happy ending."

"Oh, yeah?" she asked, glancing his way with big eyes. "What happened?"

Beckett glanced into the stall, spotting the dark bay filly drinking from the mare. "This mare lost her baby two weeks ago."

Amelia placed a hand on her heart. "Oh, no. That's terrible."

Beckett agreed with a nod. "Nash offered her as a nurse mare in hopes we could find her an orphaned foal. This sweet little babe was rejected by her mother, so she came in the other day and our girl, Nelly, took the baby on like she was her own. She's a good mom."

Tears were in Amelia's eyes as she looked back to the mare. "You're right. That is a sad story with a happy ending."

Beckett found himself lost in Amelia's heart. In his younger years, he never appreciated that heart for how special it was. Never realized how few women held pure gentleness and a nurturing soul. He imagined Amelia would act like Nelly, warm and affectionate, making her children feel loved.

Christ, he'd give everything he had for a chance to see her with his baby in her arms. Not getting too far ahead of himself, he cleared his throat and motioned to the tack room next to the feed room. "Let's get going."

She smiled. "Okay."

In short time, they had the horses brought in from the field, tacked up, and were soon atop their backs and riding past the barn out to the meadow. Beckett glanced next to him, finding a peaceful expression on Amelia's face as she rode Larry, who plodded along through the grassy meadows. Autumn kept next to the dark bay quarter horse, Danika, beneath him. He always used Danika to pony horses, needing a calm leader to teach them that going for a ride was a joy, not a punishment. While Autumn did well so far, Beckett kept her on the other side of Danika, away from Amelia and Larry. He kept a close eye on her, giving her corrections when she went too fast or became nervous and unsettled. Though Danika, a boss mare in the field, taught Autumn more than Beckett ever could.

As he and Amelia rode in peaceful silence, he thought about their relationship. Never in a million years would he have thought he'd gotten so far with Amelia so soon, which begged to question whether her feelings for him weren't as buried as he thought. He knew when they'd broken up, he'd given her no other choice than to walk away from him. There'd been no joy in his life back then, only anger for all that had been stripped away. Not only the loss of his mother and grandfather, but his purpose. He'd lost sight of his dreams. While he considered going back to the rodeo a couple years ago, he didn't have the money to support himself like he would have when he was younger and could have lived with his grandfather while he got going in the rodeo circuit. So, while he'd found peace that he'd given up that dream and found a job he truly loved with Nash, he hadn't found peace with Amelia. He'd shut her out, along with everything else that he once loved.

Once they settled back into a walk from a trot, he couldn't take his eyes off Amelia's beauty, his breath trapped in his throat. He studied the delicate lines of her cheekbones, the final hour of daylight hitting her, highlighting all the golden hues in her ginger hair. But it was the steadiness of her gaze that caught him up. She'd always given him that look when she had something on her mind. "Deep thoughts?" he asked.

She blinked, obviously coming out of whatever spell she'd been under. She met his gaze with a warm smile. "Seems to be all I do lately."

"Want to talk about it?"

Her gaze held his. "I think the question is, do *you* want to talk about it?"

A sharp iciness hit his gut at the firmness in her stare. Toward the end of their relationship, he'd been closed off and shut down whenever she wanted to talk about things going on in is life. He'd never make that mistake again. "There is no question that I won't answer," he told her. "But I reserve the right on when I choose to answer it."

She considered, resting her hands on the pommel of the saddle. "Okay, that's fair."

He inclined his head. "What's the question, then?"

"When did you become like this?"

He lifted an eyebrow. "Like what exactly?"

"At peace."

He knew the line he walked. He couldn't throw too much at her. "Some of the changes are simply growing up and maturing, I think. But the biggest changes in my life happened a month after you left for school."

"What happened?"

"Everything changed after you left." Beckett made the slight correction to Autumn, as Danika pinned her ears, curling up her nose as the mare got too close. With the horses settled, he blew out a long breath and allowed himself to go back to the darkest time of his life.

*Beckett squeezed his skull, hoping to ease the hard throbs in his head. His mouth was bone dry. His stomach queasy. He forced himself to open one eye, realizing he wasn't at home. He was lying on Hayes' couch in his living room. He peeled open another eye, and when the room stopped spinning, he also realized he wasn't alone.*

*Hayes sat on the recliner in the corner, fury written into every hard line on his face. "Beckett," he said.*

*"Mornin'," Beckett groaned. He sat up, noticing the glass of water with two pain killers waiting for him on the coffee table. He tossed back the meds, and his stomach nearly rejected the blessing.*

*"Everyone has a rock bottom," Hayes said the moment Beckett set down the glass. "This is yours. You've hit it. There is nowhere else to go but six feet under." He hesitated, and then his voice softened. "You have become the one thing you swore you'd never become." Beckett steeled himself, but he still wasn't ready for the blow, "You've become your father. You've got no joy in your life, no happiness, not a damn thing."*

*Beckett forced himself to hold Hayes' gaze, even though everything inside of him felt weak and broken and he wanted to curl up into himself.*

*When Beckett stayed silent, not having words to explain, Hayes continued. "Do you have any recollection of what happened last night?"*

*Beckett fought through his hazy memories. "I remember going to the bar."*

*"You don't remember the fight?"*

*A quick look down revealed scraps on Beckett's knuckles, and now aware of it, the corner of his lip felt sore. It occurred to him then that the pain in his head wasn't only from a hangover. "A fight? Shit, no, I don't remember that."*

*Hayes exhaled a long breath, shaking his head slowly, his lips pressed into a thin line. "Everyone has told me to stay quiet. To let you figure this out. But I can't keep doing that. Not anymore. Why are you destroying yourself?"*

*Beckett stared into his best friend's eyes, saw the warm affection there. The only affection he had left in his life. He barely managed, "You know why."*

*"Because you lost Amelia?"*

*Beckett let silence be his answer.*

*Hayes growled, "That's a fucking cop out, you know that."*

*The fury in Hayes' voice snapped Beckett's gaze up, and his friend glared fiercely. "You haven't lost shit. You let her walk right out of your life because you're too damn afraid to face the shit in your past and to deal with your father. So, now, you're drowning yourself in booze and giving up. Tell me why."*

*Beckett forced his voice through his pained throat. "She deserves better than me."*

*"Then be better. Do better." Hayes tapped the side of his head. "Get this better, so when she comes home, you're who she deserves."*

"So, that's exactly what I did," Beckett said, accepting the coldness in his chest at the memory instead of pushing it away. But pride was in there too that he could talk about this now and he'd done the work to heal very broken parts of his soul.

She watched him with big eyes. "You bettered yourself for when I came home after school?"

He nodded. "Yeah. And each day I got better. I go to therapy. Not as much now, only when I need to work through something. But back then, I talked through the accident and losing my mom and grandfather. The loss of not following through with the rodeo. Then we worked through my dad's depression, and we found a way to deal with him by distancing myself emotionally but still being there for him." He watched her expression closely, and she had her emotions very much in check. "Does that scare you to know that I was that broken?"

"Scare me?" she asked, glancing down at Larry's head, as if mulling it over the idea. She finally met his gaze again and gave a soft smile. "No, Beckett, that doesn't scare me. I'm really proud of you for doing what was good for you, and I'm so glad you pulled yourself out of that dark time."

God, her heart warmed the hell out of him. He let silence come between them as he found Autumn now walking calmly next to Danika, with her head down, her gait slow. Horses fed off the humans they encountered, and he wondered if speaking of his weakness had helped calm her insecurities too. He hoped that was true. When he glanced back at Amelia, he found her staring right at him.

Her voice cracked. "Did you think I thought you were broken?"

"I wasn't sure," he said with a shrug. "But I wouldn't have blamed you if you did."

"I never thought you were broken or weak," she said immediately. "I just didn't know how to reach you after the accident. You were so…"

"Distant. Cold. Pushing you away," he finished.

She nodded, her eyes welling before she glanced away and breathed deep. She stayed quiet for a long while, the horses' legs rustling the tall grass they walked through before she broke the silence. "I wonder what would have happened if you hadn't pushed me away."

He gave a knowing smile. "Luka wouldn't have existed in your world."

Softness reached her gaze. "I suppose that's probably true."

He sensed all the things hanging between them. All the promises he could make now and never break. "But Luka did exist," he added, unable to hide that particular truth, because if he learned one thing from therapy, it was he couldn't hide from the truth. It drowned a person to hide away, just like it was drowning his father.

"You're right, he did," she said with a sigh.

Though Beckett saw something unexpected in her expression. Not sadness. Not anger. But resolve, and nameless things he couldn't identify.

Obviously done with the heavy talk this evening, she finally let out a long breath and then sent a smile that tripped his heart. "Tonight, we're having a big family dinner, would you like to come?"

Beckett smiled, a deep hole in his chest mending a little. He was getting this right with her, and it made the years of facing his pain worth it. "I'd love to. Nothing beats dinner around the Carters' table."

She returned the smile and then glanced out at the Colorado beauty ahead of her. Until she suddenly gasped, "Shit!"

Autumn spooked. Beckett quickly settled her and then turned to Amelia. "What's wrong?"

She slowly looked at him, giving a wide grin. "Those beer samples, the ones I've been struggling with?"

"Yeah?"

Her eyes danced. "I think you've just given me the answer I've been looking for." She spun Larry, clicked her tongue, and took off cantering toward the farm.

Autumn began prancing, and Beckett chuckled, shaking his head. He did what he felt like he'd been doing since the day he met her outside of their high school. He chased after her.

## 9

Back at the house, sitting around the large picnic table they always used for big family meals, Amelia felt... *different.* Everything felt different now. When she'd decided to move away to college, she secretly hoped that Beckett would reach out for her and that she'd get him back, but it never happened. Part of her felt sad for all he'd gone through, but the other part of her realized that if her leaving meant it helped him get healthy, it was worth it.

As she looked around, her chest felt open and so full of love... It had been years since she'd been this comfortable at one of their family dinners. She knew why—Luka wasn't there. The biggest truth that hit her was she realized, that while embarrassed over being dumped by Luka at the altar, that emotion was nothing in comparison to the pain she felt when Beckett had pushed her away. That was love. What she had with Luka wasn't the same. She pushed around the baked beans on her plate, wondering why it had taken her so long to see that something was wrong between them. It made her wonder, after Beckett shared his truth, if she'd been hiding from hers. All she and Luka had done was fought, and if she were honest, she had her doubts about him for a long time. In the broken parts of her heart, she knew she'd been so desperate to make it work with Luka, because she didn't want to fail at love twice. She'd put up with the fighting, always having a way to explain it away. She overlooked the way he never took any interest in her life, and how he turned his nose down at her small town life.

Someone kicking her foot had her lifting her head. Beckett's brows were knotted. "You okay?" he mouthed.

She nodded and gave him a smile to reassure him.

It didn't work. His brows tightened further.

She stared into his strong, solid eyes, losing herself in all they offered her. With all the honesty bubbling up, she began to realize that this was what she had truly wanted. The ease Beckett brought. He'd grown up with her sisters. They were all close, Clara's protective nature of Beckett proving that. But she knew now, surrounded by her family, both blood and chosen, that Luka had been a fill in. Luka was the guy she thought she wanted because the one she craved had been unattainable. But Beckett was no longer pushing her away. He wasn't cold. He wasn't distant. And her heart knew the man locked onto her like she was the only thing he could see at the table, passion, desire and sweet things pooling in his eyes.

At whatever showed on her face, emotion filled Beckett's expression. The world faded away as he reached across the table, taking her one hand in the both of his. In the space between them, a connection bloomed that seemed tangible in the warm air.

"Um, well, this got weird," Maisie said.

Amelia blinked, startled, as she suddenly remembered they weren't alone. Every set of eyes were locked onto her and Beckett. She tried to pull her hand away, but Beckett held on tight. When she met his gaze again, she read his expression, knowing it from the years they had together. *I got this,* those steady eyes told her.

Beckett threw Maisie a sly smile. "Weird is my walking in on you buck naked dancing around Hayes' kitchen."

Maisie blushed up to her eyeballs, and Hayes barked a laugh. "Ha! I'll never forget that." He slapped the table. "The look on both your faces. Classic."

At the end of the table, sitting next to Clara, Mason burst out laughing. "Auntie Maisie was buck naked."

"That isn't funny," Clara chided her son, but she looked to be fighting her laughter.

Maisie sighed, leaning over to Mason and said, "It is a little funny, but that's not a story you tell your friends. I have enough embarrassment from that day."

While everyone joined in the conversation and the laughter, Amelia couldn't look away from Beckett as he lifted her hand to his lips, and looking right at her, kissed her palm. She'd felt this with him before. Happiness, not jaded by any hurts. She forgot how nice this felt. How real and honest and true, and how Beckett knew her heart, understood what she needed when she needed it. How had she forgotten that?

When he finally released her hand, he gave her a little smile that stole the air from her lungs. A smile that was all for her, *only* for her, as Clara blessedly changed the topic. "How are the new beer flavors coming?" she asked.

Amelia gently pulled her hand away, still feeling his kiss on her palm. She spotted the glimmer in Clara's eyes. She obviously didn't hate what happened between her and Beckett. Amelia began to wonder if both her sisters knew what Amelia had just realized a second ago. "Actually, today I had a little bit of a breakthrough when Beckett and I went out for our ride and he was talking about sitting around our dinner table." When silence greeted her, she laughed. "Do you want to hear my ideas?"

Next to Clara, Sullivan wiped his mouth with his napkin and nodded. "Who better to run your new beers ideas than your number one fans?"

"Well, funny you should say that," she said. "Because you're all inspiration for the flavors."

Maisie set down her BBQ rib onto her plate, scrunching her nose. "What do you mean?"

"Honestly, I was drawing a blank coming up with fresh ideas, and today it just hit me. Foxy Diva was all Pops, so I drew inspiration from all of your personalities for the new samples." To Maisie, she said, "Take you for example, your beer is a dark ale. It'll taste like white peaches mixed with bananas and summer fields."

Maisie rubbed her tummy. "Sounds delicious."

"I think so too," Amelia said with a laugh. To Hayes, she said, "For you, we've got an amber ale, with flavors like second cut grass, sour crust dough and a hint of banana to sweeten things up."

Hayes grinned, about to bite into his rib. "Now that's a beer I can get behind."

She smiled at him before turning to Sullivan. "You're a Pilsner full of soft grain, a hint of orange, gentle spice and hay."

"We all know that beer will hit it right out of the park," Sullivan beamed.

Hayes snorted. "Terrible pun. Just God awful."

Everyone around the table laughed, as Amelia said to Clara, "Yours will be fresh Indian pale ale, with white wine, gooseberry, papaya with lime."

"Ooh," Clara said. "A perfect beer for a summer's day."

Amelia agreed with a quick nod then sent her smile onto Mason. "For you, buddy, since you love Christmas so much, I thought we can do a Christmas Ale, with flavors of candy canes, honey and light spice."

Mason grinned big. "Does that mean I can drink it?"

"No," Sullivan and Clara said in unison.

Mason pouted at them but said to Amelia, "I love candy canes."

"I know you do," Amelia replied. "You can eat all the extra pieces."

"Did you hear that, mom?" Mason asked. "Auntie Amelia said I can eat all the pieces."

"Within reason, of course," Clara said.

Mason gave a little glare. "*All* the pieces, Mom."

Laughter followed again, and Amelia smiled at the sweet sound.

"What about my beer?"

Amelia met Beckett's gaze, consumed by how he watched her. How maybe he always watched her, and she never noticed because her focus had been elsewhere, in the wrong direction. "You're a dark ale. Chocolate, coffee and caramel." Her three favorite flavors.

His sweet smile said he knew it too.

"I think this is an amazing idea, Amelia," Clara said, scooping up more beans on her spoon. "Each one of those beers sound incredible. I've got no doubt that Ronnie will be thrilled and they all will, as Sullivan says, hit it out of the park."

Sullivan gave her a kiss for that.

Amelia nodded. "At least we have a way forward now. We're competing against some talented Brew Masters to get that spot, but I feel good about it." Or at least felt good about having a plan since she'd been running on empty for ideas.

Maisie smiled. "Sounds like a good plan."

Mason asked, "When do I get my candy cane?"

Clara pointed her fork at his full plate. "How about you worry about this food instead?"

Mason shrugged and began digging in. Sullivan smiled at

his son before he said, "It's really amazing what you've done. The three of you. Pops would be so damn proud of you all and your brewery."

Clara smiled and nodded, pride bursting out of her. "He truly would. I don't think he ever could have imagined when he left us his inheritance and the property that we'd ever get this far with his favorite beer."

Maisie beamed with light, as always. "Nah, I think he knew. He always seemed to know what a force we were when we put our minds to something."

"I think you're right," Amelia said. Her gaze slipped away from her sisters landing on Beckett. His gentle smile greeted her. She smiled back, knowing that while the brewery would make Pops happy, her spending time with Beckett again—a guy that Pops truly loved—would delight him even more.

LONG AFTER THE kitchen was cleaned up and the house was quiet, Beckett inhaled Amelia's vanilla scent before he wrapped his arms around her from behind. So many wonderful memories were held in his house. Amelia's grandfather, Pops, had been the best man that Beckett had ever known, other than his own grandfather. Pops had accepted Beckett into the family with open arms and put him in his place whenever he deserved that too. Sometimes, life simply wasn't long enough, and Pops deserved more time. "Thank you for dinner." He dropped a kiss on her neck and smiled against her soft skin when she shivered. "You've really become quite the cook."

"You're welcome." She spun in his arms and pressed her hands against his chest. "It was nice having you here for a big family dinner."

"It's been a while," he agreed. While he did see Amelia

whenever the group got together, he skipped family dinners whenever she and Luka were around. He hadn't trusted himself not to slam his fist in the prick's face. Hayes had told him the stories of how Luka talked to Amelia. How they fought. How he treated her with little to no respect. Beckett wouldn't have been able to handle that. "So, Miss Amelia, what would you like to do this evening?"

She gave him a cute look. "Actually, I have a really fun idea." She took his hand and he followed her out of the kitchen and up the staircase.

When she entered her bedroom, he grinned. "I'm liking where this is going."

She laughed softly. "*That's* not my idea."

He took a step toward her. "Bet I can change your mind."

"Oh, no," she said, holding up her hand, slowly backing away. "You wait right there. If you touch me, I'll get distracted." She spun quickly and headed for her closet, which had an old door with a vintage keyhole. After she grabbed something out, she turned back to him and held a shoe box. She took a seat on her bed, and he joined her right as she opened the box.

One look inside at the contents and his heart flipped in his chest. "You're kidding me?" He reached inside the box, taking out a photograph of them in his old beat-up 1970's bright blue Ford. He'd loved that truck and had driven it until it died on an old country road. "Jesus, look at us, we were just kids."

"I know, right? We look like babies, and to think we thought we knew it all back then." She reached in and took out a stack full of photographs from the time they started dating right up to just before she left for school. High school football games, prom, summer parties, every moment of their lives were right there in the box. "Look, this is the movie stub from our first date."

"You kept this?" He took the ticket and examined it. He'd taken her to see scary movies at the old theater in town that had been demolished a few years back after the property was sold.

"I kept everything," she said, with a certain sweetness in her voice. "All of it. Every little bit of our life together."

He studied the contents, spotting the little notes he'd respond to when she'd pass him in the hallway before he graduated a few years before her. Everything was there. All of their adventures, their happy memories, and even the harder ones, when Beckett looked thin and tired.

When he glanced up at her, he found tears in her eyes, "Every man that I dated after you had to compete with this." She waved out to the box. "All these wonderful memories."

"They were good," he agreed.

"Good and near impossible for anyone to compete with," she said, gathering up the memories and placing them back in the box. "Because how can someone compare to something that's perfect?"

His breath hitched at the emotion on her face and in her voice, even in her words, as she rose and stood next to the bed. It took all of Beckett's strength not to reach for her and claim her, but he wouldn't rush her. He didn't want to miss a moment of the way she watched him, so lovingly, so open, like tomorrow and every day after it, she'd always look at him like this.

He grew hard when she reached up and slid her shirt over her head, leaving her in a white lace bra he wanted to rip off her. "But you still remember exactly how to touch me," she said slowly, stepping out of her jean shorts. "You always did know me better than anyone else."

"Because I was the first one to touch you," he managed, need flooding him, thickening his voice. "We taught each other what feels good."

"Yes, we did." She held his stare in a way he hadn't seen in a very long time. The veil of distance had been broken and all the love between them flourished again.

Consumed by all she offered, he rose on trembling legs. "You've got to stop looking at me like that."

She pressed her hands against his chest, pouring heat into him. "How am I looking at you?"

"Like I can have all of you," he murmured. "I'm trying to do the right thing here. Be what you need me to be. But I have my limits."

Her eyes searched his, intensity blazing in their depths. "What if I said you can have all of me?"

He froze, his muscles quivering. Years he'd waited for her to look at him like this. To have a single moment when she saw all of him. And there, she was, *his Amelia.* "I don't want to disappoint you," he managed.

She unhooked her bra, letting it fall down her arms, and then removed her panties.

His hands clenched into fists. His gaze roamed over her, every spectacular inch from her light pink painted toenails, up her toned legs to the ginger curls between her thighs, to her rounded belly, to her rosy, taut nipples, and then past her parted lips, begging for his kiss, to her half-lidded eyes. He swallowed. Deeply.

She stepped closer, until all her softness pressed against his hard planes. "Well, you're not intending to disappoint me, are you?" she asked, staring up at him with glistening eyes.

"No, I'm not," he said, roughly.

"Then I think we're done talking." She slid her touch across his cheek and cupped the back of his head, pulling him down to meet her mouth.

Any control he had left snapped at the feel of her heated kiss. Between their open-mouthed kisses, he rid himself of his clothes before gathering her in his arms. Once he laid her out on her bed, he settled between her thighs, gazing upon the soft curls between her legs. He didn't hesitate, driven by desire he could not control. His hands shook with adrenaline as he dropped his head between her thighs, desperate for the taste he'd longed for. He groaned as he slid his tongue across her slit, tasting her arousal when she moaned deeply. Well aware how she liked his mouth on her, he licked her again, lighter this time, teasing and tempting her.

She moaned again, dropping her head back, and he reveled in the way she trembled. He reached for her breast, holding her tight in the way she'd always loved.

Another moan, and she ground her heat into him. She smelled like Amelia, a scent belonging only to her, sweet and so seductive, the aroma drove him to forgo his idea of teasing her. He focused his tongue on her clit, swirling, nipping, sucking, until she lifted her hips off the blanket beneath her.

"Oh… don't… stop," she gasped.

He nearly laughed at the thought but was more deter-mined to get her there. "Do you want to come, Amelia?" he asked.

"Yes," she panted.

He nipped her clit, and her legs began to shake. "How long has it been since you've found pleasure like this?"

A pause. "Since you."

"Good." He settled his mouth over her clit again and slowly inserted one finger, then two. He worked his fingers, slowly, but eagerly, her whimpering making him throb to slide deep inside her. When she soaked his fingers, ready and desperate, he took her over the edge.

One hard suck later, and a round of fast thrusts of his fingers, and she was coming against his tongue, wildly bucking against him.

Her musky scent enveloped him, and he gathered a condom from his wallet when she urgently opened his jeans and shoved them down over his ass. He groaned at the feel of her trembling hands, understanding her need. She took the condom from his hand and had him sheathed a moment later.

He moaned against her mouth as she slanted hers over his. He'd waited years for *this*. Her unabashedly wanting him, driven crazy by lust that she jumped off the bed and pushed on his chest, sending him walking backward until his legs hit the bed. He sank down on the mattress, gathering her in his arms until her knees were on the bed and the tip of him was inside her.

She broke the kiss, her intense stare on him, as she slowly lowered herself down on him, inch by inch, her eyes widening the deeper he went. And Christ, he went deep. His cock pulsated at the tightness of her, the wetness, as she worked herself down on him until he was balls deep. His moan echoed hers as she shifted her hips, back and forth, her head falling back.

He caught her taut nipple between his teeth, sucking the bud up to the roof of his mouth. She began grinding against him, circling her hips, until she had him throbbing. He nipped the taut bud, and then he caught her moan in his mouth. He sucked on her tongue, tasting every bit of her mouth in the way he knew she liked it.

She worked her hips harder, back and forth, grinding herself atop him. "I know what I want now, Beckett."

He nipped her bottom lip, then grabbed her hips, stopping her. "What do you want?"

"You," she whispered.

His heart tripped. He grabbed her hips tight, and done with hiding all that he felt for her, he gathered her in his arms and flipped their positions. Staring down at her beauty, her hair laid out beneath her head, her creamy flesh all his to explore, her beautiful, sweet eyes only on him. He cupped her neck, while his other hand went to her thigh, pushing it back, letting him slide back inside her as deep as he could. "Are we doing this then, Amelia? Me and you? We're trying this again?"

She cupped his face. "Yes. I want that. I want you."

She might have said more, maybe even had conditions to how this would go between them, but he didn't let her finish. He *couldn't* let her. Overcome with a reality he never thought possible, he didn't take for granted their joining. He unleashed his strength, claiming what had been his from the first day he'd touched her. With every touch, he removed any memory of another man on her body. With every thrust, he made a new memory she could keep forever, just like all the memories in her shoe box. He gave her everything he had to ensure she always knew what this felt like. And as he roared his climax, his semen exploding from his cock, he knew one day, he'd do just that without a condom, and make the family that they both deserved.

"I seriously have no idea how you can eat so many pancakes," Amelia said, placing another stack of pancakes onto Beckett's plate the following morning.

He began pouring maple syrup overtop until it dripped down the sides. "Easy. When they taste this good, keep 'em coming."

She slid the spatula back onto the empty plate. "Well, sadly for you, you ate them all."

He shoved his fork into the stack and began cutting. "There's always tomorrow," he mumbled before taking a huge bite.

She laughed, moving back to the dishwasher and adding all the dirty dishes inside. Birds danced through the outside of the window, the sunny day their playground. She realized as she cleaned up that having Beckett there this morning reminded her of how full the house once was, not only when Pops and her grandmother were alive, but when Clara, Mason and Maisie lived there too. Mornings were always so loud and busy. She liked having someone to cook for again.

Once she closed the dishwasher, she moved onto her next

stage of her plans this morning. Beckett always handled tough talks better after he had food. She took the piece of paper she'd left in the drawer, then slapped set it down next to his plate.

His fork clanked against the plate at his check presented to him. "I don't want that."

"Yeah, well, I don't want the check either, so we're at an impasse."

He ignored the check and rose, adding his dishes to the dishwasher. "I've said it before, and I'll say it again, that was not your debt, Amelia. Put it in your account." He turned to face her, his gaze cold and flinty. "If you refuse to do that, I'll put it in myself."

Yeah, she could play tough guy too. She crossed her arms. "Then I'll redeposit the money into your account."

He snorted a laugh, and it didn't sound amused when he gathered her in his arms. "The only person you're going to annoy by doing that is the bank teller. This is a battle you will not win. I cannot live with myself knowing that asshole has your money. Please stop fighting me on this."

Understanding his point, but knowing she needed a loophole because she couldn't live with herself knowing he'd paid Luka that much money, she gave him a quick kiss and settled back at the sink.

As she set the pan in the drying rack, strength and warmth engulfed her again as Beckett embraced her from behind. "Thank you for breakfast," he murmured in her ear. "Tomorrow it's my turn to cook for you."

Her eyes fluttered, heat building at all the places he touched last night and this morning. She forgot about these little things that used to be so easy with Beckett. She forgot what it felt like to be with someone who made it a point to talk about all her good qualities, instead of always wanting her to change into something else. "You're welcome." Hands still soaking wet, she turned around, sliding her arms around his neck.

He held her close, his gorgeous smile better than any coffee to get her going today. "What's your plan today?"

"I need to get started on brewing those sample beers and hope to hell they turn out," she said.

His hands slid around her hips to tuck into the back pockets of her shorts. "How long does that process take?"

"If I nail it the first time, not long, but I never nail it the first time, so I'd think a few days to get the ingredients right." She paused, considered the work ahead of her and then shrugged. "I suspect some will be easier than others."

"Anything I can do to help?"

The heated smile he gave had her moving a little closer. "What you're doing for me right now is more than enough."

His chin dipped, his mouth mere centimeters from hers. "Which is?" he asked roughly.

"Making me happy."

"Then I'm doing something right," he said. He slanted his mouth across hers, and his kiss was sweet, only at first. The force of his embrace kept building. His hands squeezed her bottom before moving back up until he gathered her shirt enough to sneak a hand beneath. His touch felt like fire.

Desperation began to crawl through her as heat simmered low in her body, need building and building, and the only way to ease it was Beckett being inside her. She ground against him, and his answering low groan rumbled against her lips. He grabbed her by the waist and hoisted her onto the countertop. His kiss dragged from her mouth to her cheek to her neck where she moaned, dropping her head back as he relentlessly devoured her until she was eagerly pulling him forward for more. Everything felt like it made sense now. She wanted *this*, Beckett's touch. She definitely did not have everything figured out—nowhere near it—but for all the bad in her life, she wouldn't turn her back on something that felt so good. And Beckett's touch was out of this world. She moaned, arching into him as his fingers tangled in her hair and he angled her head, deepening the kiss. There was absolutely nothing gentle in his touch. Nothing soft in how he unbuttoned her shorts and had them down to her knees. Nothing easy about the way he shoved up her top and her bra, exposing her breasts until he roughly squeezed each one, leaving her gasping.

"Is this what you were looking for, Am?" His voice rumbled by her ear, and she shuddered, desperate for him to fill her.

"Yes," she managed. Her eyes fluttered into the back of her head as his mouth met her neck, his teeth her shoulder.

She lost herself as his strong hands encased her, stealing every thought from her head as he ground himself against her, the hardness of his cock a tease she couldn't possibly endure. "I want you inside me."

His low chuckle tickled her ear. "Better give you what you want, then."

She shivered as he backed away and yanked the front of his T-shirt over his head, tucking it behind his neck. Then he squeezed her breast, leaning down to deeply suck on her nipple. The heat of the burn shot through it, remarkably building more heat between her thighs. He gestured at her shorts. "Take those off for me." With shaky hands, she wiggled out of them, along with her panties, until she sat before him naked, her breasts exposed, her sex his to take. He groaned. "Fucking hell, Amelia, you're so damn pretty." His mouth met hers again, and he took her breath away with a knee wobbling kiss that caused heat to pool in her core.

She heard the rattle of his belt buckle, the *thud* of his wallet hitting the floor and the crinkling of the condom wrapper open all before she heard the clicking of his cowboy boots as he moved in closer to her. The heat of his body and the strength of him infused the air as he captured her chin in his grip.

His low groan shivered down her spine as he slid between her thighs, finding her soaked and ready with his hand. He growled in her ear before he was filling her. Inch by inch, he stretched her until she was utterly filled by him.

His hand slid to the back of her neck, holding tight, but the grip felt right, dominating in the best possible way as his other hand gripped her hip. And something even more than that. Something so familiar and perfect and safe that she never wanted to let go of it. He pulled back, inch by inch, just as slow, letting her body mold to him. And only when he moved in slow and easy, both their soft moans echoing each other, did his fingers tighten on her neck and hip.

Then he unleashed himself.

His intensity felt like years' worth of buildup and desperation on the very edge of exploding. She bit her bottom lip, desperate to keep from screaming against the pleasure pulsating within her. Her legs began trembling with the force of his cock pumping hard and fast inside her, building more and more pressure until those trembles turned into hard quakes.

"You're quivering on me," he growled against her mouth. "It's so damn hot."

"Please," she managed.

His thrusts never stopped, one after the other, driving up into her, as one hand came to her breast. His fingers tight against her nipple. The other hand went between her thighs, the pressure she craved suddenly met by his finger pressed against her clit. She froze against the intensity, and she fell into his touch.

All that pleasure built to uncontrollable limits, and she clenched her teeth, sex, *everything* against the rising euphoria.

He grunted. Deep. "Jesus, you're tight. Fucking hell…"

But she wanted her turn. She pushed on his chest, sending him back and jumped off the counter, spinning around, remembering how much he used to like taking her from behind. She heard the low rumble from his chest at the view of her wiggling hips. He slid behind her and she found the tip of him, and she slowly took him in, inch by inch, his throaty moan echoing hers.

She sensed him widening his stance as she began to move, slowly dragging herself over his smooth hardness. Until she found a rhythm that brought pleasure. Skin slapped against skin, and their moans danced together as she took him deep. She sped up, moving harder and faster, but failed to get there. She whimpered against the rise of the pleasure, but the cliff was so far away.

A deep grunt rose from low in his chest before he slapped her bottom, bringing more heat to where she wanted to soar. She gasped as he threaded his fingers in her hair, pulling her head back so he could murmur in her ear, "Finish with me."

Then he did the most unexpected thing of all, he unleashed himself in a way she'd never experienced before. Not with any man, not even with Beckett before. Pounding thrusts had his sac brushing against her, pleasure building in places she didn't know pleasure belonged.

His fingers tightened on her hips, and he went even harder, sending her right over the edge, shattering her body until she couldn't remember where she began and he ended. His cock grew harder and bigger inside her, making her eyes water as the pleasure became blinding as his thrusts became harder. Faster. Urgent. Wild. Yes, this felt good, anything this good couldn't be bad, couldn't be wrong. Beckett was big, filling her, stretching her, and when as he went faster and harder, becoming unhinged, his raspy moan echoed hers.

Until there was no beginning to the pleasure and no

ending, only wave after wave of pure satisfaction as she broke apart around him, vaguely aware of his bucking and jerking as he followed her over the edge.

Then the doorbell rang.

"Shit," she breathed.

He nipped her shoulder, still deep inside her. "We can ignore it."

The doorbell rang again.

"I'm expecting a delivery today for ingredients for those samples," she said. He cursed and slowly withdrew. She spun around and quickly dressed, but first enjoyed his desire-filled gaze. "More later," she told him, when he silently watched her with a heated stare, burning her up where she stood.

His brow arched. "You bet your pretty ass we'll do this again later."

She questioned her sanity walking away for *that* when she hurried to the front door. She got there on the third ring, but nothing could have prepared her for who stood on the other side.

"Hey," Luka said.

She noted the bruising still looked terrible, and his nose was in no better shape. "Luka, um, hi," she managed. But in that second of seeing him again, everything felt wrong. She felt wrong. The pain on his face felt wrong. The shame in his eyes felt *wrong, wrong, wrong.*

The door was gently taken and pulled back as a re-dressed Beckett settled in next to her, wrapping an arm around her shoulder. "Hello Luka," he said, cool and collected, even though his gaze was deadly. "What brings you by?"

Luka went ghost white. He glanced between Amelia and Beckett before he cleared his throat and said clearly, "I came by to let you know that I dropped the charges." To Beckett, he added, "I did that for her, not for you."

Beckett snorted. "You did that so you could take her money, don't kid yourself."

Luka's lips parted, but Beckett turned his back to Luka. Surprising her, he took her chin and kissed her. Not a small peck goodbye, but a hard, dominating kiss that left her a little winded when he backed away. "I'll see you later."

Amelia wobbled a little. "Um, yes, okay, see you later."

She couldn't see Beckett's expression, but by the way Luka took a step back, she assumed he'd perfected his death glare.

Silence remained until Beckett drove down the driveway and then Luka turned her way again. He shoved his hands in his pockets, barely able to look her in the eye. "I just came by to tell you that and to thank you for the check again." He gave her a quick look. "I wanted to tell you in person."

It wasn't *just* for that. She read what he needed in his pained eyes before he walked down the porch steps. Suddenly, everything became so clear. What felt so wrong earlier now made sense. His sadness, culpability was all wrong. "You were right, you know," she called.

Luka froze. He glanced back over his shoulder "Right about what?"

"Us," she explained. "There was something wrong there for a long time. It wasn't just you who felt that way." He turned to fully face her, color returning to his cheeks, hope slowly filling his eyes. Deep in her heart, she knew she had to do this for him, and for her too. "I think I didn't want to believe it, or I had been blind to everything that had been going with us, but I guess what I'm saying is…" She could hardly believe what she was about to say, "…thank you for stopping the wedding. Thank you for stopping what would have been the biggest mistake of our lives."

Luka's shoulders sagged, an obvious heavy weight lifting from him. "You mean that?"

She nodded. "Do I think the way you ended things was right? No. But endings are hard. Emotions are messy. I just don't want you thinking that you were the only one to blame for all of this. My fault lies there too." Everything settled in her mind as she decided the best way forward through all of this for herself and for Luka, a man she had cared about deeply, was to tell the truth. "My heart was never yours to have."

His brows knotted. "What do you mean?"

"It's a long story," she told him. "Do you want to hear it?"

"Yeah, I do," he said, with a soft smile.

After spending ten minutes on the phone with his criminal lawyer, Beckett now knew for certain that Luka dropped the charges. Even with this good news, Beckett's mood was shot. Things were going well with Amelia. Really well. If that prick got inside Amelia's head and undid all the healing they'd been through, Beckett might do something to make those charges return. He'd spent the remainder of his morning with Autumn, tacking her up and working her with the saddle on in the round pen before he spent a good hour on groundwork to deepen their bond. He'd known cowboys to use force, but he never saw sense in the method. All his preparation and groundwork was to build trust. If he did that right, she'd have enough faith in him to ride her and stop giving him grief. Right as he wrapped up, giving Autumn a hose off to cool her down before returning her to the paddock, he received a text from Hayes: Up for wings and beer for lunch?

Beckett removed Autumn's halter and she wandered over to her feeder full of hay. He shut the gate behind him and fired off a text: Meet you in fifteen.

Nash never minded if Beckett took a longer lunch, and right now Beckett needed to talk to his friends and get his head straight.

The drive into downtown took longer than expected due to a three-car collision on the country road into town. By the time he arrived at Kinky Spurs, a western-themed bar belonging to Nash's wife's, Megan, he found Hayes and Sullivan already seated at a table. Megan was behind the shiny, reclaimed-wood slab bar when he arrived. She had distinctive eyes—the left one blue, the right one brown—and her long, sandy-colored hair held a slight curl. He gave her a wave, which she returned, and then continued to show a new employee around, or so Beckett assumed since he'd never seen the twenty-something guy before. Customers sat around squared tables and in booths; the ones closest to Beckett arguing over the best soccer player in the league.

"Hey," he said, his chair scuffing against the hardwood floors as he slid it out. He took a seat next to Hayes and across from Sullivan. He noticed the Foxy Diva already waiting for him, and look a long, long sip, relishing in the crispness. "Thanks for ordering the beer."

"No worries," Sullivan said with a laugh. "I was too damn thirsty to wait." He lifted his beer and tipped it toward Beckett. "Gotta get a few more of these in before I head back to Boston."

"Are you leaving soon?" Hayes asked.

Sullivan nodded. "In a couple days for some team meetings and press, but then I'll be back. How about we talk about your face."

Beckett lifted his brows. "What's wrong with my face?"

"You look miserable," Sullivan pointed out. "What's up?"

"Luka is what's up," Beckett grumbled. When both his friends frowned at him, he set to explaining. "The prick came by Amelia's place to tell her that he dropped the charges against me."

Hayes whistled. "Oh, yeah, what did you do when you saw him?"

"Kissed the hell out of her in front of him," Beckett said, with a smile he suspected looked deadly.

Hayes barked a laugh. "Good for you, and even better the charges have been put to bed."

Beckett agreed with a nod, right as Megan sidled up to the table.

"Wings all around?" she asked.

"Always," Hayes said, as they never seemed to order anything else. Kinky Spurs had the best wings in River Rock.

"Excellent," Megan said, clearing away Sullivan's and Hayes' empty beer bottles. "Another round?"

"Yeah," Sullivan said. "Put this one on my tab."

"Will do," Megan said. "Wings coming up shortly."

"Thanks," Beckett said to her, watching her walk away and wondering if Nash had found his relationship with Megan so complicated when they started dating. He figured everyone had their ups and downs, and he looked back at Hayes and Sullivan, who watched him eagerly. "What?"

"There's gotta be more going on here than Luka showing up," Hayes said. "Considering how chummy you and Amelia were last night at dinner, how are you not riding a serious high right now?"

Beckett blew out a low breath. "When Amelia saw Luka at her front door, she looked like she was about to puke."

"Not surprising," Sullivan remarked. "He dumped her at the altar. It can't feel good."

"No, it can't," Beckett muttered, picking at the label on his bottle. "I just hope that bastard doesn't get in her head and mess up all the progress we've made. I finally have her back in my life, and this fucking guy just won't go away."

Hayes leaned in, his brows drawing together. "You think she might get back with him?"

"It would be foolish of me not to consider that risk," Beckett said, relaying the thought that had been on his mind all morning. "She was with him for three years. He proposed. She accepted. Obviously, she loved him."

"Last night, it sure looked like the only man she was thinking about was you," Sullivan offered.

Beckett inclined his head. "And yet, this morning when we saw Luka, she looked ghost white."

Silence was his friends' response, and Beckett took that to mean his concerns were valid.

Customers on the far side of the bar suddenly roared as someone scored a goal in the soccer game playing on the big screen monitors. When Beckett looked back to the group, he found Hayes smiling brightly at something over Beckett's shoulder. Only one thing made Hayes smile like that.

Maisie sidled up to the table, her expression looking as pissed as Beckett felt.

"That's not a happy face," Hayes commented, grabbing Maisie by the waist and pulling her onto his lap. "What's wrong?"

"Luka is what's wrong." She slid her gaze to Beckett, pity in her face. "He's at Amelia's, and I wish I had the ability to make him vanish off the face of the earth."

"You and me both," Beckett agreed.

Maisie's eyebrows shot up. "You knew he was there?"

"Yeah," he replied. "I was there when he showed up this morning."

"Why didn't you make him leave?"

Beckett gave a dry laugh, slowly shaking his head. "Have you met your sister, Maisie? If she wanted him gone, she would have gotten him to leave."

Maisie huffed, crossing her arms. "I don't like it. Fine, he comes to, I don't know, make amends or whatever shit he thinks he's doing, but why does he need to still be there? What in the hell are they talking about?"

At that, a chill ran down Beckett's spine. He glanced down at his watch. Two hours had gone by since he'd left her house. He met Maisie's gaze again. "He's still at the house?"

"Yeah, he's been there a while from what I hear," Maisie grumbled. "Clara told me they've been talking. I seriously don't know why she gives him a second of her time. What else do you need to talk about other than to tell Luka he's an asshole and to never come back to the house?"

Beckett absorbed what he heard and looked between Hayes and Sullivan. Both his friends wore matching deep frowns, and Beckett knew now for certain his concern had some merit. He wouldn't lose her. Not to that fucker. Never again.

He rose, and Hayes lifted his brows. "Where are you going?" he asked.

"To make sure she's all right," he said.

"Is that wise?" Hayes asked, his voice shifting into the authoritative tone he used on the job. "The charges have *just* been dropped. Sit down. Take a breather. Contact her later."

Beckett shut his eyes, fighting against the draw to ensure no one else got close to her. But he didn't want to get any of this wrong. He let out a long, stabilizing breath and then reopened his eyes, returning to his chair.

"Smart decision," Hayes said, right as Beckett's cellphone vibrated in his pocket.

When he pulled it out, he noticed the call was from an unknown caller. "Hello," he answered.

A soft voice on the other end of the line asked, "Hello. I'm looking for Beckett Stone? Is this him?"

The spicy aroma of hot wings infused the air as Megan

carried over a tray and began setting down the plates. "Yes, it is. How can I help you?"

"Mr. Stone, I'm afraid I have some difficult news to tell you…"

The world faded away, his heartbeat hammering in his ears the only sound he could hear. His stomach rolled, his chest aching for air as he shot up from the table and ran for the door, hearing his friends yelling after him.

❧

LATER THAT AFTERNOON, Amelia rubbed at her aching back, examining her work for the day. The three one-gallon glass apple cider jugs were now full of sample beers and fermenting. She'd made Beckett's beer, Hayes' and Clara's. Tomorrow she'd get to the other three. In two weeks, she'd know if these beers were a disaster or something brilliant. And hopefully out of the six, Ronnie liked a few of the samples.

"It smells good in here."

Amelia glanced back, finding Maisie and Clara behind her. Someone was missing though. "Lots of brews make for yummy smells. Where's Mason?"

"Raiding your fridge," Clara said with a smile. "Are you all done here for the day?"

"Yeah, everything on my body hurts and my brain is mush," she said, removing her apron and leaving it on the hook on the wall. "Have either of you heard from Beckett? He's not answering my texts."

Maisie cringed, slowly raising her hand. "I might have something to do with that."

"Why?" Amelia asked, suspecting she wasn't going to like the answer.

Maisie twirled from side to side, nibbling her lip. "I met up with Hayes and the guys at their lunch earlier. Hayes and I were going to do some shopping after they were done."

"Okay, and…" Amelia pressed.

Maisie winced and said in a rush, "Well, I was annoyed that Luka was here talking to you for so long, and Beckett was having lunch with Hayes and I just blurted out that it bugged me you and Luka were talking."

Amelia sighed, calculating the time from when Beckett left to when Maisie met up with him at lunch. She and Luka had talked… for hours, in fact. "I wish you hadn't said anything," she told Maisie. She probably only added fuel to Beckett's irritation. "Was he upset?"

"I mean, not really, but kind of," Maisie said.

Clara snorted. "That is not an answer, Maisie."

Maisie shrugged, unable to meet Amelia's gaze. "I just mean that he didn't look thrilled you were speaking to Luka still, but he wasn't all in your face angry about it." She hesitated then looked up at Amelia through her lashes. "He kind of took off."

Amelia sighed and took her cell from her back pocket, waving it at her sister. "Maybe angrier than you know since he's not returning my texts."

"Maybe," Maisie said, hunching her shoulders. "I'm sorry. I was just venting. He said that he knew you were with Luka, so I didn't think I would ruffle any feathers."

"He did know that Luka came over today," Amelia explained, catching hints of the cocoa extract lingering in the air. "He was here when Luka showed up this morning. He just didn't know that Luka had stayed that long."

Clara crossed her arms, pinching her expression. "Well, what happened?"

Amelia rubbed at that continuing ache in her back and gave a small smile. "I think this conversation needs some margaritas." Their go-to drink whenever a talk got heavy.

"I'm so in for that," Maisie said, and took off toward the house.

Clara and Amelia followed her inside. When they made it to the kitchen, they'd also discovered that Mason had indeed raided her fridge and tore through the house, making messes wherever he went. The fridge was left open, the cupboard where the crackers she kept stocked for him was ransacked.

"Mason, get in here right now," Clara snapped.

Loud footsteps came thundering from the family room where the Avengers movie they'd watched a thousand times together was playing. "Yeah?" he asked with a full mouth.

"Are you a tornado?" Clara asked firmly.

His little dark eyebrows furrowed, and he looked so much like Sullivan when he said, "No, I'm a human."

Clara pointed to the cracker cupboard. "Then clean up the mess you made right now."

As fast as he probably entered the kitchen, he had cabinet doors slammed and was heading back to watch his movie.

Clara sighed and shook her head at her son. "Little boys are exhausting."

Amelia laughed, definitely feeling for Clara. Mason was more than a handful and seemed like his power switch was on lightspeed mode. Amelia reached for the margarita glasses in the cupboard as Maisie mixed up the drink. Once Maisie poured them, they headed out to the back deck where Amelia had recently bought some updated patio furniture to have a seating area that was shaded by the mature tree next to the house.

She took a seat on the couch and took a long sip of the margarita. First hit by the sugary sweetness on the rim of the glass, followed by the tangy lime juice with a hard hit of the tequila. Maisie always made the drinks strong. "I don't even know where to start," she admitted, resting her glass on the armrest.

Clara took the spot next to her. "How about at the beginning?"

Maisie flopped onto the big couch, crossing her ankles onto the coffee table. "Or at least where things got interesting."

Amelia laughed softly, thinking back to her conversation with Luka this morning. "Is telling Luka that he was right to call of the wedding interesting enough?" Both her sisters' mouths dropped open, and Amelia laughed again. "Guess so."

"You'll have to explain this to me," Clara said, breaking the thick silence, "because I can't see beyond him being a total asshole for what he did to you."

Amelia tucked her legs underneath her, noting the calmness in her heart. "Okay, sure, the way he called off the wedding was horrible, but I get why he did it. We did get wrapped up in the wedding, all of that. The truth is, I should have ended things with Luka long before he did, and that's on me."

"Because you weren't happy?" Maisie asked, like she already had figured out what took Amelia a long time to come to grips with.

"Because my heart was already wrapped up in someone else who I never got over." There, she said it aloud. She waited for the world to come crashing down, but it never did.

A soft expression reached Clara's face. "I think we all know you and Beckett are the real deal," she said.

Amelia agreed with a nod, feeling like she was finally on the right track, and she was ready to let life take her when she needed to go. "I can't even explain it all, nor do I have it all figured out, but when I went to college, it was just so different from life here. I liked that. You know, being someone different. Especially because back then, I lost Beckett. I didn't even know him anymore. He went from this guy with a promising rodeo career ahead of him, who loved me madly, to someone else." Her sisters knew her pain back then. The heartbreak she went through as she tried and tried and tried to make things work with Beckett, but he'd been so lost back then, so unreachable. He wouldn't talk about anything, share his feelings, let her in. Until she couldn't live like that anymore, and decided college was her way out. "When I came back from school, I never let myself look too closely at him, knowing I couldn't, knowing the risk, knowing that all I'd want was him."

"But then you did look at him?" Maisie asked.

Amelia nodded. "It's like he's back to himself. Open, willing to talk about us *and* himself, and to share in my life and let me share in his."

At whatever crossed Amelia's expression, Clara cocked her head. "Isn't that a good thing?" she asked, before sipping her drink.

"It's incredibly good," Amelia confirmed, running her fingers up and down the stem of her glass. "But today I shared that same type of thing with Luka. We were just honest. We talked about all the feelings we had for each other at the beginning of our relationship. We talked about how simple life was while we were in school. We were the same, wanted the same things, did the same things, even. But when I moved back home, I became the old me, the country girl, the one who doesn't want a big city life. And that's when we drifted apart, but he was too proud to end the relationship. I think I was too afraid to fail at another one, especially right in front of Beckett's eyes."

Maisie finished her sip. "So, your talk was all about healing, then?"

"It was," Amelia agreed with a soft nod, squinting against

the sun peeking through the trees leaves. "I think we needed to give each other permission to admit that we were no longer in love, and that was okay."

Clara blew out a long breath, crossing her legs. "Luka is lucky to have your kindness, and I'm happy you made peace with all this. Does this mean he's gone from your life?"

"Yup," Amelia said. "We hugged, wished each other well, and I doubt I'll ever see him again." Which felt weird—she'd been with him for three years. But then it didn't feel weird either. The final goodbye felt right. Good.

Maisie swatted at a fly and asked, "Does this mean you and Beckett are moving full steam ahead?" Maisie asked.

She nearly said *yes* but stopped herself short. "That's where things get a little complicated," she admitted. "If I learned one thing from talking to Luka today, it's that I finally feel like I know who I am. I know what I want. And I want Beckett. We were great in high school, but now we're adults and we still work together. Even better than before. Yes, there is a lot of messiness and hurt in our past. A lot of history. A lot of pain. A lot of healing. But I want to be with him and work through that with him." She hesitated and drew in a long deep breath before continuing. "I know Beckett and I have gotten back together quickly, and I know I should feel embarrassed and weird about that, but I don't. It feels good. Right."

Clara took Amelia's hand, squeezing tight, giving a soft smile. "I'm proud of you. You've handled all this with such grace."

Maisie agreed a nod. "Hell yeah, you have."

"We're here for you, all the way through this," Clara said. "All we want is for you to be happy."

"Thank you," Amelia said, and then laughed. "All I want is to be happy too."

"Amelia."

The cold dread in Hayes' voice had Amelia shooting straight up from her seat, her heart leaping in her throat. "What's wrong?"

"It's Beckett," Hayes said slowly, his dark eyes troubled. "His father died."

In the cold, lifeless, yellow-painted hallway of the hospital, Beckett pressed his crossed arms tighter together as the middle-aged doctor across from him spoke words that Beckett had a hard time processing. Her nametag read: DR. HOLLOWAY. He stared into her stern, light blue eyes before glancing at her thin mouth, focusing harder on her voice as she said, "Did you know your father had heart disease?"

"No," he answered. "He never shared that with me." But Beckett wasn't surprised. His father shared nothing. They talked sports, weather, and the news, and not much more than that.

Dr. Holloway's expression gave away very little. "Your father came in about a month ago with shortness of breath. I offered advice on his care, but he denied any further help. Were you aware he came into the emergency room?"

Beckett shook his head. "No, he never said anything, but he'd never been a fan of hospitals."

"I see," Dr. Holloway said, pressing the chart to her chest

between her folded arms. "Seeing that he has a history of heart disease, it is unlikely an autopsy will be performed, unless you formally request one. If the request is denied, you can privately have one done, but they are pricey."

"I don't want an autopsy done," Beckett muttered, his stomach rolling. "If you say it was heart disease, I believe you."

Dr. Holloway inclined her head in agreement. "I suspect that is the case, yes. Are you comfortable sending your father to River Rock's funeral home?"

"That's fine," Beckett agreed, the walls in the hallway moving closer and closer until they felt like they were squeezing him from both sides. "Is there anything else I need to do?"

"Not at this point," Dr. Holloway explained. "The funeral home will contact you tomorrow to discuss your father's arrangements and the steps you need to take for his estate."

Pain hit the back of Beckett's throat as he stuck out his hand. "All right, thank you for your guidance, Dr. Holloway."

Dr. Holloway returned the handshake. "Again, Mr. Stone, I'm terribly sorry for your loss."

Beckett feared opening his mouth again, not sure what would come out of it. He simply nodded and then watched the doctor walk away. His legs trembled, so he took a seat in the hard, cold plastic chair in the hallway of the hospital wing. He tipped his head back and closed his eyes, trying to control the pain ripping through him. Life was cruel. He was finally getting his life back together, and right as that happened, death came back. *Again.*

"Beckett."

He shut his eyes tighter against the sweetness in Amelia's voice. He didn't want her to see him like this. The years he spent in therapy to gain control of the fury, the despair, the pain to ensure he'd never lose sight of himself again. Because in his mind, he thought if he got strong again, life would finally cut him a damn break.

When gentle hands gripped his arms, he couldn't stop from opening his eyes. A sweet angel, she was the only damn good thing he'd ever done, and even that he couldn't get right. Amelia knelt on her knees between his legs, her soft eyes on him. "I'm so sorry," she said, tears in her eyes.

Beckett's gut twisted. "I had no idea this was coming…"

Her grip tightened like that hold could take away the darkness invading his thoughts. "What happened to him?"

He explained what the doctor told him. "He had ordered groceries yesterday," Beckett managed through a thick throat. "The guy who delivered them today had instructions to bring them in through the back door. When he got inside, he found my dad on the floor, unconscious."

"He called the ambulance?"

Beckett nodded. "When I arrived, they had him on a ventilator, but the doctor told me there was no brain waves or signs of life, so I gave them authority to take him off life support."

Amelia's fingers dug deeper into his arms. "Oh my God, Beckett, I'm so sorry you had to make that decision."

Beckett looked to her fingers, seeing the force in which she held him. He should feel that, he realized, feel the pinch of her fingernails digging into his flesh. He felt nothing but a cold void.

When he looked up into her eyes again, a tear streamed down her face. "Your poor dad."

Like an elastic band snapping, the cold void vanished to hot fury. "No, not my poor dad. He did this to himself by sitting around and not living anymore, not taking care of himself."

He hated the way her brows lifted. "Maybe that's true, but no one deserves to die alone. No matter how much he gave up on life, he didn't deserve that."

A wave of icy despair hit him right in the chest, and he felt his stomach heave to rid itself from his body. He saw the way his anger shocked her, and he hated himself for it. "This shit never ends." He pressed his fists against his eyes, fighting against the battle cutting through him. "Why does this shit never fucking end?"

"It's not fair," she said, clutching like she was scared he'd fade away if she let go. "It really isn't fair."

He dropped his hands, finding her gaze locked on him. Christ, how good she was, all loving, with a soul blindingly bright. His hand shook when he cupped the side of her face. "You of all people know how unfair life can be." She'd lost her parents, then her beloved Pops. Tears fell from her cheeks, and the sight ripped his heart out. He cursed fate for always throwing sadness into their lives, when all he wanted was to do right by her. To take all the pain away that she'd already endured. To not allow death to touch her life again, or to let her see the darkness simmering inside him, the weakness. "I need to handle the arrangements and get his estate figured out. I'm going to need you to give me a few days to get this sorted out."

She leaned into his touch, pressing her hand over his, offering him her whole heart in that single embrace. "You don't have to do this alone. Let me do this with you and be there for you."

He didn't want her near this, near him while he buried his father. "I can't..." He swallowed deeply, shaking his head, feeling the anger roaring beneath the surface. And the worst part was, the last thing he wanted to do was talk to his therapist about the shit he felt right now. Feeling like he hung from a thin thread, he said, "I'm not in a good headspace right now. I need you to trust me that I have to do this alone."

"Beckett, you're being silly," she said. "Let me help you through this difficult time."

The gentleness in her voice ripped his heart out, and he pushed his own desires aside to keep the promise he made to himself a long time ago. "When I started to get better during therapy, I promised myself that if you ever let me back into your life, that none of this dark shit would ever touch you again. I lost you once because my pain devoured me, and I couldn't see a way to make sure that didn't affect you too. I can't see through anything right now. All I can focus on is the anger I feel roaring through me. I won't break that promise, Amelia. I can't."

She drew in a sharp breath, leaning back on her legs. "Please don't shut me out again. I can deal with anything, but I can't deal with that."

"I'm not shutting you out. This isn't the same thing. I just need to get my head together." Barely able to stand the way she watched him with emotion-packed eyes, he rose, and she released him, but she didn't rise. "I'm sorry, Amelia. I need time. Please give it to me." He nearly walked by her but stopped, forcing himself to speak his truth and turned back to her. Tears ran down her cheeks and the sight nearly sent him to his knees as the walls began to get closer and closer, until he could barely draw air through his lungs. "I can't hurt you again. Not like before. I can't let my pain affect you. Please understand, I need to deal with this alone."

"Beckett," she whispered, her chin quivering.

He saw the pain rippling on her face. The agony she endured realizing that the past was touching them again. That no matter what he did, this hell followed him, and he couldn't keep her safe from it.

"I'm sorry." His throat squeezed tight as he pressed a kiss to the top of her head, and then he did the only thing he could do, he walked out of the hospital and prepared himself to bury another one of his family members.

13

One week had ticked by slowly, and Amelia had felt each second of those days, knowing that Beckett was facing his father's death alone. She'd texted and called him daily, but he never answered her calls and only texted a few words back to let her know that he was doing all right, but busy with all the paperwork and details for his father's estate and funeral. Nothing more. Nothing less. Her head and heart were an equal mess. She and Luka were in a good place, but what she felt with Beckett now was all too familiar. He'd shut her out after his mother and grandfather passed away, and they were right back to that again. Part of her understood. He kept his father separate so it didn't affect his life, of course she got that. But there was a deep part of her heart that knew not being involved wasn't going to get them anywhere. Especially since it felt like Beckett wasn't facing his trauma, he was once again avoiding it. Her heart balked, knowing what happened the last time he did that. He turned away from her, and she couldn't even fathom that happening again. Only she had no idea how to reach him.

Over the last week, her brewery had never been cleaner. All she'd done was clean between creating the final three beer samples. She did her best to keep her mind and heart busy. But it didn't help. Nothing helped. And after eating breakfast this morning, and feeling very much alone, lost in her thoughts and ready to crawl out of her skin, she called in reinforcements.

"Margaritas?" Amelia asked, glancing over her shoulder to her sisters who were talking about Mason's latest art project at school while sitting around the kitchen table.

"Sure, I'll make them," Maisie said, jumping up from her seat.

"I'm right here," Amelia said, waving Maisie off. "Sit down. I'll make them."

Maisie's lips parted, but Clara interjected, "Actually, it's probably best if I don't have one." She hesitated before the brightest smile rose to her face. "I found out yesterday that I'm pregnant."

"Oh my God," Maisie exclaimed, her hands covering her mouth.

Bursting with happiness, Amelia rushed to Clara's side and threw her arms around her older sister. "Congratulations, Clara. This is so exciting. I had no idea you were trying."

Clara returned the hug, squeezing tight. Her voice filled with wonder. "We weren't actively trying, but I've been off the pill for a while now. I honestly had no idea. I spotted a little with my period this month so didn't think anything was up, but the other day, I don't know, I just had a feeling and got a test." When Amelia leaned away, she found tears in Clara's eyes. "Both Sullivan and I are really happy."

"Does Mason know he's going to become a brother?" Amelia asked.

Clara gave a quick nod. "Since I knew I was coming here

and planned on telling you both, I told him before he went to school. I knew once he got there, word would spread quickly."

Amelia laughed. "I'm sure it will. He'll be such a proud big brother."

Clara agreed with another nod, glancing at Maisie, who still gaped at Clara. "I'm starting to think you're not happy about this news. Why aren't you saying anything?"

Tears filled Maisie's eyes, her chin quivering. "I am happy. It's just… well, I guess now is the right time to tell you that I'm pregnant too."

Clara gasped. "For real?"

Maisie nodded, tears streaming down her cheeks. "Only *just* pregnant. I took the test last week before we last had drinks together. The line on the test was faint, but yesterday, the doctor confirmed we're expecting."

Clara's elated expression shifted, her brows drawing together. "But you were drinking that day last week."

"No, I wasn't," Maisie said, with a sheepish smile. "That's why I jumped up to make these drinks too. I didn't put any alcohol in mine."

"Smart," Clara said, opening her arms wide. Maisie stepped into them, and they hugged tight. "Pregnant together," Clara continued, awe in her voice. "How much fun will this be?"

"So fun," Maisie agreed.

Amelia absorbed the news, the happiness on her sisters' faces. A sudden wall of emotion hit Amelia, nearly knocking her over, tears welling in her eyes, her sisters blurry in front of her. Her cheeks burned as the room began to spin. She grabbed the back of the chair, holding tight, and at the small squeak that escaped her, both of her sisters looked at her and immediately rushed to her side.

"Shit," Maisie snapped, grabbing Amelia's arms. "We shouldn't have said anything."

Eyebrows gathering, Clara's mouth downturned. "Sorry, that was totally insensitive."

"No, it's not insensitive at all," Amelia said, her breath catching. "It's really great news, and I'm so happy for the both of you. These aren't sad, pitiful oh-poor-me, tears."

"What tears are they, then?" Maisie asked, pulling Amelia toward the chair.

Amelia took seat, swiping at the tears on her face. "It's just that, I'm taking in all this good news and thinking how incredible it is that with all the loss we've had in our lives, that now, all this good is happening. How happy our parents would be to see you two so happy. How happy Pops and Grandma would be."

"You're right, they would be happy," Clara said, dragging the other chair across the hardwood floor to sit next to Amelia. "It feels like there is a *but* in there."

Amelia's chest squeezed tight as she looked between her sisters, and realized a hard truth. One she'd been running from for a long time. All she wanted was to have that kind of happiness with Beckett. To be his wife. To have his children. And to find that everlasting happiness that wasn't surrounded by so much death and misery. Her heart only and always wanted *him.* But all of those dreams were slipping away from her fast, and she felt like she was scrambling to hold onto them. "I just can't help but wonder when is Beckett's time to be as happy?" Her throat tightened with the emotion squeezing her. "When does Beckett get these happy moments like Hayes and Sullivan have found? When does he get to be showered with all the goodness life has to offer? When does he get to stop surviving, but truly living? It just makes me so damn sad for him."

Clara's eyes saddened. "He's definitely had a hard time."

"He has," Amelia said. "And I have no idea how to help him. Even after all this time, I still don't know how to reach into his heart and make everything better. And once again, he's shutting me out. It just feels like we're back to square one. I thought we'd grown so much since then."

Maisie said, "You should read Pops' letter."

"Pops' letter?" Amelia asked, leaning against the counter.

"Yeah," Maisie said with a nod. "The letter that Pops left you in his estate, read that."

Gosh, Amelia had forgotten all about the letter that had been in his Last Will and Testament. Each letter was in a sealed envelope with their names handwritten by Pops, and in each was a quote. One last piece of advice.

Amelia looked to Clara, and she shrugged. "It actually did help me a lot."

"Well, right now, I'll give anything a shot." Amelia moved into the dining room, and in the hutch's drawer, she took out her letter. When she returned to her sisters, she opened the envelope and read the note.

*"So we beat on, boats against the current, borne back ceaselessly into the past." -F. Scott Fitzgerald*

And with those few words, it was like Pops was whispering in her ear. She saw the quote differently now than when she'd read the letter after Pops passed.

Maisie asked, "So, by your face right now, this means something to you?"

Amelia's hands shook and she set the paper down on the counter. She knew exactly why Pops left this quote for her, and her heart warmed. "It's means that Beckett and I have been rowing boats against a rough tide, but no matter where we go, we are always brought back to where we started. Our past. We can't outrun it." Amelia swallowed back the remainder of emotion tightening her throat. She drew in a big, deep breath, sending the rest of the rawness in her chest away, thinking only of Pops now and of his wonderful love. So many conversations, hard and easy, they shared around this table. So many truths were told, no matter how hard they were to admit. So many tears shed and so many smiles had. Her heart opened in ways it never had before, under Pops' love and last final piece of advice. "But we can turn the boat around and go in another direction, a better tide, a smoother one." Amelia's heart swelled, her way forward so clear now. "From the moment Beckett punched Luka in the face, he's been fighting for my love and protecting my heart."

Clara cocked her head. "What are you thinking?"

"I'm thinking that maybe it's about time I do the same."

⚓

BECKETT'S EXHAUSTION felt soul deep, eating away at dreams and hopes. He felt the same thing after his mother and grandfather passed, and again when depression stole his father away. While Nash had told him to take time off work, Beckett needed to get his mind off the stabbing pain in the center of his chest. Especially considering this afternoon, while looking through his bank records, he noticed that Amelia had cashed his check. Nothing felt right. He seemed lost without her at his side, and yet, he didn't want her anywhere near him. Until he could sort out why the loss of his father had him spinning out of control, he needed to stay away. He knew he was pushing her away again, and he hated himself for it. But more than that, he knew he needed to protect her. He would figure out his emotions and then he'd go back to her. He just needed a little more time. He settled the bridle on Autumn's head and stroked her neck. "Today's the day, girl. I need this ride as much as you do. It's time to take a leap of faith."

She rubbed her head into his shoulder, and he hoped that was a good sign.

Beckett left the fence where he'd been tacking her up and brought Autumn into the middle of the ring. She stood patiently, calmly, as he tightened the cinch. Before he slipped his foot in the stirrup, he exhaled slowly, letting go of the tension simmering through him. Only when his felt his muscles loosen did he swing his leg over the saddle and take up the reins, and then he waited for the explosion. For the second she decided he wasn't worthy to remain on her back, but as the seconds ticked on, he never felt her tense up or take a wrong step. He gave a click of his tongue, the same click he'd used when he'd been moving her out on the ground. She walked forward with ease, her gait steady and unhurried, her head low, jaw relaxed. Another click from his mouth, and she stepped up into the trot, and not long after that fell into a lope. Beckett didn't mess with her, didn't fuss with her mouth, he let her enjoy the ride. When he felt comfortable that she wasn't going to hurt him or herself, he called, "Whoa." She slowed back to a walk, and he steered her to the gate and bent over to unlock it. Once through, he directed her past the house to the field where the brood-mares had recently been living. The land was flat, and the grass was short.

Autumn's walk became more animated with each step, obviously feeling Beckett's excitement. By the time they headed through the gate, Autumn was bouncing in a trot, a feeling akin to being in the gate before the calf was sent out and he'd burst out with his rope ready. He missed that feeling, that adrenaline. "All right, Autumn, let's see what you've got little lady." He released the tension on the reins and Autumn shot forward, like she'd done this a thousand times before, galloping toward the mid-day sun, stealing Beckett's heartache as she went.

By the time they returned to the farm, Autumn's walk was quiet and slow, and Beckett felt the smile rise on his face, enjoying the joy she'd brought him. He quickly untacked her and then hosed her off before letting her loose in her paddock again.

"She's fast as hell."

Beckett glanced over his shoulder at Nash. "Shockingly fast."

Nash studied Beckett's face before he crossed his arms. "She looked good. Great job with her."

"She needs more training," Beckett said. "But she's got heart, and a lot of it."

Nash agreed with a nod, then gestured to Beckett's truck. "Since I already told you not to come in today, I'll say it again. Go home, Beckett. Now's the time to be with friends, and that's not a request."

Beckett watched Nash return to his house, and knew Nash meant well. Everyone meant well, but being home was the last place Beckett wanted to be. This morning, he poured all the booze he had in his house down the sink and threw out the bottles, not trusting himself not to drown his sadness in the bottle, just like his father. He felt unsettled, restless, and wasn't sure how to gain his footing again.

Autumn gave him a final look before she settled in front of her hay, and he got into his truck and hit the road. They had a way to go before he'd end their training, but today went better than he could have anticipated.

The drive home was quiet, he left the radio off. His window was rolled down, and the warm breeze brushed scents of wildflowers and summer days against his nose. When he arrived home, the lightness in his chest from the ride with Autumn sank as he found Hayes and Sullivan sitting on his porch. He'd been dodging their calls, dodging life, and he knew it.

Beckett parked his truck and got out a second later. "I thought you were heading back to Boston?" he asked by way of greeting, approaching his house.

Sitting on the porch in the old worn wood chair, Sullivan shook his head. "Coach gave me the go-ahead to stay until after the funeral."

"You didn't have to do that," Beckett said, taking the seat next to Sullivan.

Sullivan snorted. "Hate to break it to you, brother, but you're not going to that funeral alone."

Beckett knew he should thank him, but he simply looked toward the trees, the empty fields, the empty barn, where once there was so much life. "The funeral is tomorrow."

"You arranged all that, then?" Hayes asked.

Beckett nodded. "It's simple. It'll be at the cemetery. Nine o'clock."

"We'll all be there," Sullivan said.

*Amelia will be there;* he didn't say it, but he implied. Beckett knew nothing he could say would stop that, so he gave a small nod.

Silence settled in, but it wasn't comfortable. Beckett knew what was coming long before Hayes said, "She's hurting as much as you are right now."

"I know she's hurting," Beckett replied. "You don't need to tell me that."

Hayes leaned against the railing, arms crossed, voice firm. "If you know, then why you aren't doing something about it?"

Beckett sank his head back against house, his bones aching with the tiredness seeping through him. "It will always touch her."

"What will?" Hayes asked.

"The pain. The goddamn curse on my head. The misery that's following me."

"Beckett," Hayes said, slowly. "Bad shit happens. You know that, I know that." Yeah, Hayes did know that well—his first wife, who had been Maisie's best friend, had been murdered. Hayes understood deep loss. "But good things can come from the bad experiences too."

"When?" Beckett asked, the same question he'd been asking for his whole damn life. "When do the good things come, Hayes?" It occurred to him suddenly what was grating on him. Maybe somewhere in his messed-up head he thought his father would come around and see the light, but now that would never happen. All there was in his past was pain. "It doesn't matter what happens, this shit comes back. Time and time again." He ran his hands over his face, feeling his muscles quivering. "I kept thinking that all this time all I needed was to get her back. To be better for her. To do better. But I can't outrun the truth that when I heard my father died, all I felt was weak and broken."

Sullivan's chair creaked when he leaned forward to cup Beckett's shoulder. "That's expected. Fuck man, anyone would feel like that."

"I can't even look her in the eye right now," Beckett said. "I made a promise I wouldn't hurt her that way again, I won't break that promise. I just need to get past this."

"You're going to lose her before you get past this, Beckett," Hayes shot back. "Do you fucking hear yourself? You finally have her back. Keep her. You need to let her in."

Beckett hated how pathetic he sounded when he said, "I can't risk fucking this up again. I need to get my head on straight, and it's all the fucking way crooked right now. I can't let her see me like this again."

One second he was sitting in his seat, the next, Hayes had him up against the wall, his fists tight in his shirt. "Wake the fuck up, Beckett," Hayes roared, spittle forming in the crease of his mouth. "I refuse to let your fucking father destroy you.

147

That's the last deep cut he's leaving, and I won't stand by and watch you walk away from your chance of being happy."

"Let me go," Beckett said, slowly, carefully, the back of his head throbbing from hitting the wall.

Hayes' glare only intensified. "Your grandfather would be so fucking ashamed of you right now. So furious that you're letting the disease your father spread across your life affect you like it is now."

Sullivan sighed. "Guys, sit down. Both of you."

Hayes ignored him, his neck corded. "Maisie's pregnant, and we've just learned today Clara is pregnant too. How do you think that made Amelia feel when she learned the news?"

Needing space, feeling the air thicken around him, Beckett shoved Hayes away and moved to the railing on the porch, gripping the wood tight beneath his hands. "I know exactly how it made her feel. Like her chance of having children was slipping away from her. Because I'm pushing her away. *Again.* I fucking know."

To calm down, he let out a long slow breath, nearly congratulating them, but Sullivan cupped his shoulder and said, "It's time for you and Amelia to get married, have some kids, live a goddamn happy life."

"It's not that simple," Beckett said.

Hayes growled from behind him. "Why is it not that simple?"

"Because I'm not you," Beckett snapped in return. To Sullivan, he said, "Or you. I'm not fucking good at this. I've never been good at this. I don't know how to do happy. I thought if something bad ever happened again, I would know exactly how to handle it. But I don't. Happiness never fucking lasts."

Hayes jabbed a finger at him. "Guess what, Amelia doesn't want me or Sullivan, she wants you. Not the perfect you. Not the man holding back to take every step just right. She wants the man she fell in love with. All the good bits and the broken and the weak."

Sullivan gave a slow nod. "That's the good stuff, man. When they see all of you but want you anyway."

Beckett glanced away, feeling each word, albeit each forceful word from Hayes, and the gentler ones from Sullivan. These men were his brothers, and his head suddenly began to clear as each word cemented. He glanced over his shoulder at Sullivan and then to Hayes. "Why would she want a part of this?" He tapped the side of his head.

Hayes expression softened, as he stepped into cup Beckett's shoulder. "She's wanted you from the day she met you. I saw back then, and I see it now."

Beckett felt something break inside him, but it didn't cripple him, it opened a doorway to another way forward. "I'm going to lose her?"

Hayes gave a firm nod. "You're going to lose her if you keep her out of your life again, so what are you going to do about that?"

Beckett glanced out at the farm again, the land of his grandfather. "I best figure that out before she's gone forever."

14

---

The next morning, Amelia exited Sullivan's truck fifteen minutes before nine o'clock, and her heart shattered. Standing next to the casket suspended atop the grave was Beckett, his head bowed as he waited next to the minister. He wore black dress slacks and a navy-blue button up with a black tie, and the minister next to him was in a full black suit with a tie. Her mouth went bone dry as her high heels sank into the grass, her heart reaching for his. Becket had never looked more alone, only making her realize exactly what she needed to do next. Not only for him, but for *them*.

"Here are the flowers, Auntie Amelia," Mason said, wearing khaki shorts and a white dress shirt. He offered her the wreath of white roses, lilies and carnations that she picked up from the florist this morning.

"Thank you, buddy." She dropped a quick kiss on the top of his head, which he did his best to avoid, running back to Sullivan and Clara as they waited for Hayes and Maisie, who were approaching from their truck.

Today, even the universe seemed to understand that

Beckett needed more light. The sky was a stunning blue, and with the light breeze, the air was rich with floral scents from all the flowers left around the gravestones. She inhaled the beauty, reminding herself that even though this place was hard for her to visit, today wasn't about her or her loss. Leaving the others at the trucks, Amelia approached, and Beckett's gaze met hers. Dark shadows lived in the depths of his gray eyes that looked so much darker today, and she suspected the darkness there wasn't only about the loss of his father, but that he'd walked away from her in the hospital and had shut her out. But she was done with feeling hurt or confused. She knew what she wanted, the answer all too simple with Pops' last bit of advice. *Beckett.*

For years, she'd run from her feelings, and avoided truly letting herself feel the heartbreak of losing Beckett. She'd simply left home, moved on, but failed to ever truly leave him behind. Because the truth was, there was no moving on from Beckett. He was her life, and she wasn't going to run away from that any longer.

She walked between the headstones, too familiar with the area. To her right, at the very end of the cemetery beneath the huge shade trees was where her parents were buried, along with her grandmother. Pops' ashes had been spread on the property, where he wanted to stay forever.

When she reached Jim's casket, she placed the wreath on top and then placed her hand on the shiny wood, saying a little prayer for him before moving to Beckett's side. She glanced his way, finding his head bowed again, and she didn't hesitate in sliding her hand in his. His eyes slowly shut, and she heard his rough breath. Her guts twisted when he opened his eyes and tears were in them. She held his hand a little tighter.

As Beckett's chosen family formed a circle around the casket, the minister began the ceremony and said, "Today we gather to celebrate the life of Jim Stone. We gather to share the pain..."

The ceremony continued, but Amelia couldn't really hear the words, she could only see the pain rippling on Beckett's face as each second went by. Brutal pain, cruel pain. She wished they didn't have this in common, but she understood that heartache. Death wasn't kind. Death was swift and cold. But she'd seen the other side; the bright side, where life got better, where smiles felt real and honest, and laughter overtook the misery.

Amelia only refocused on the minister when he asked, "Would anyone like to say a few a words?"

Beckett didn't even look up. "No—"

"I would," Amelia interjected.

Beckett's gaze jerked to hers, uncertainty heavy on his face. "You don't need to do that," he said, firmly.

"I know," she countered. "But I want to."

He squeezed her hand, obviously to stop her, and she squeezed back, feeling like she knew exactly what steps to take forward. She was sick of getting life so wrong. Now she listened to her heart, and her heart knew the right path to take. Her heart knew how to get Beckett's heart to hear her.

With force, she pulled her hand from his, although his hold tightened to keep her there next to him, and she settled in next to the minister. Before she began, she took out the piece of paper in her purse and looked around at her family, surprise in all of their faces. "I knew Jim before he lost his wife and after the devastating loss, and the moment I read the poem by Mary Frye, I knew I wanted to read it for Jim today." She hesitated, drawing in a deep breath, and then began reading the poem:

> *Do not stand at my grave and weep,*
> *I am not there, I do not sleep.*

*I am a thousand winds that blow.*
*I am the diamond glint on snow.*
*I am the sunlight on ripened grain.*
*I am the gentle autumn rain.*
*When you wake in the morning hush,*
*I am the swift, uplifting rush*
*Of quiet birds in circling flight.*
*I am the soft starlight at night.*
*Do not stand at my grave and weep.*
*I am not there, I do not sleep.*
*(Do not stand at my grave and cry.*
*I am not there, I did not die!)*

WHEN AMELIA LOWERED THE PAPER, she caught Beckett's soft stare locked onto her, and then she noticed her sisters were crying, wrapped in Sullivan and Hayes' arms. Everything in her heart told her this poem was perfect. She hoped—begged—that the universe would ensure this was the last time Beckett ever faced something so hard and felt alone. "It's easy to speak about why Jim doesn't have anyone else here to say goodbye to him. Why he lost all his friends, his business associates, his family. He no longer talked to anyone. But I believe that when Jim lost his beloved wife, he died alongside her that day."

The slight breeze caused the flowers on the casket to flutter, almost as if Jim was nodding in agreement. She hoped that was true, and continued, "Instead of finding the beauty and the good left in his life, Jim stood at the grave and wept. He didn't see the winds that blew. The diamonds glistening in the snow. He never felt the spatter of autumn rain again. He only saw the grave, the darkness, and could never see anything else." A pain hit the back of her throat at the raw emotion filling Beckett's eyes. She paused to collect herself before she went on, "Jim could never see *anyone* else."

A tear slid down Beckett's cheek before he wiped it away quickly. Amelia nearly sank to her knees at his despair, but swallowed her emotions needing to finish. "I was so mad at Jim for how he faded away from life. But..." her gaze fell to the casket, "I can't be angry anymore. I can't even pity him. I can only accept that he was lost without Tammy and the color had gone out of his life."

She waited for Beckett to meet her gaze again before she smiled through the tears, "I also believe now, that when the birds quietly circle in flight, that's Jim and Tammy together again. That when I'm admiring the soft starlight at night, amazed by the beauty, that's the everlasting love Jim had for Tammy. And that now, what was so wrong is made right because he's where he should have been all along. With Tammy." She stepped closer to the casket and reached down, picking up some of the dirt. "Today I choose to forgive you, Jim. Forgive you for where you went so wrong. I wish you everlasting peace with Tammy." She tossed the dirt onto the casket.

Beckett watched her closely as she returned to his side, and when she reached him, he did the most unexpected thing, he enveloped her in his arms. His head buried in her neck, and she felt him trembling. Felt his tears on her shoulder. And it occurred to her that she wasn't the only one who'd done some soul searching over the last few days. For the first time ever, he allowed her to feel his weakness, sense his misery, and be the safe home he needed when things got hard.

Locked together, the minister finished the ceremony. Amelia watched Clara and Sullivan toss dirt onto the casket and say their goodbyes to Jim, as well as Maisie and Hayes, but Amelia didn't step away. Didn't move a single inch. She did the one thing she swore she'd do from this day forward. She held Beckett tight, and let his pain bleed into her.

☙

TWO HOURS LATER, Beckett returned home after completing the final paperwork the funeral home had for him. He entered his home, comforted by the scent of leather and wood that always lingered in this house. He dropped his keys on the entryway table and headed for the living room, where he spent most of his time whenever he was here. A bank of large windows allowed natural light to pour in and the mountains off in the distance were a welcome view. He stared out at the grassy meadow, feeling an odd mix of clarity and unease, which came as a shock. He expected to feel raw after the funeral, but there just wasn't any room for that anymore. He was unsurprised when he heard the car drive up his driveway. And a warm comfort washed over him as he heard his front door open and shut and the click of high heels as she drew closer.

Then everything in his world rightened as Amelia said, "Beckett."

He turned to face her. She still wore the black lace dress he'd seen her arrive in, her gorgeous hair in wild waves around her face, her piercing blue eyes all he could see. "What you did today..." he said, his voice thick. "What you said, Amelia, I've never heard anything so beautiful."

"It's beautiful because it's true," she said, moving closer. "Because that's the way forward now. Forgiveness and peace."

He closed the distance, sliding a hand against her lower back, bringing her close against him. "Your heart amazes me," he said, tucking her hair behind her ear. "It blinds me with its kindness." Tears welled in her eyes, but he pressed on. "The way you spoke about my father today, I've never seen things that way. It made me realize that he and I are not that much different. I cannot imagine a world where you're not in it." He caught a tear on her cheek and brushed it away with his knuckles. "I don't know my way around all this, and I'm sorry I shut you out and hurt you. I want to do better. I just don't know how."

She leaned into his touch. "We can do this together. Get through this together, Beckett. When I lost my parents, I had my sisters to lean on and Pops. You don't have to face all this by yourself. You have Hayes and Sullivan, my sisters, and me."

"I do have that, don't I?"

"You do," she said, softly. "This is hard. Really hard. It's okay to feel lost and raw and not sure which way you're turning, but at the end of the day, I'll be here and you don't have to question anything or be any different than who you are, because I love you, Beckett." She fisted her hands in his shirt. "I only want you. All of you."

The coldness today brought was shattered by the warm affection in her eyes. "Say that again."

She laughed gently. "I love you."

Emotion squeezed his chest as he cupped her face. "I love you too, Amelia, and have from the day you tripped on the stairs in front of the high school and I caught you in my arms." Needing her more than ever, he slanted his mouth over hers. The kiss was soft and sweet, without any of the rawness he usually offered.

He gathered her in his arms, and she wrapped her legs around his waist as he carried her into his bedroom at the end of the hallway. When he met the mattress, he laid her out, but she sat up immediately. She pushed his shirt up, and he helped her remove it. Her fingers quickly went to work on his belt and pants as he reached behind her and unzipped her dress. He only had removed her dress over her head when he felt her damp tongue slide across his cock. He groaned, the dress fluttering to the floor as he looked down. She took him in fully, her mouth moved back and forth, dragging pleasure across him, moving slowly, teasingly. Just how he liked it. And when she licked lower, taking his sac into her mouth and sucking, his eyes fluttered back into his head, sensation sweeping him away.

Until she took him deep into her mouth again and moved faster, sucked harder, and he refused to finish this way. "I need to be inside you," he said, hearing the desperation in his voice. She gasped as he reached for her and he tossed her back on the bed. Her laughter—her beautiful laughter—surrounded him as he closed his body on hers, and she spread her legs for him, welcoming him close.

He reached for his nightside drawer to retrieve a condom when she grabbed his hand and said, "No, not today. I get the shot for birth control, and I need you, Beckett. I need to feel just you."

Urgent now, he sensed the tremble of his hand as he slid his touch up her thigh, pushing her leg back as he shifted his hips closer. A low groan escaped him as her warm arousal coated the tip of his cock as he entered her. Determined to stay as close as he could, he took her mouth again, devouring her moan as he slid all the way to the hilt. So warm. So wet. He froze, right there, letting her hold him. "There's no better feeling in the world than this right here," he murmured against her lips.

"I bet I can prove you wrong." She shifted her hips, and he sank in even deeper.

"Fucking hell, Am." He grunted against her mouth, and then he began to move, keeping his body tight against her.

She moved with him, his pelvis grinding against her with every thrust forward.

He only broke the kiss when she had trouble kissing him back, her moans echoing the slaps of skin against skin. Dropping his head into her neck, kissing beneath her ear, he laced his fingers with her hands and took them above her head, and he rode her. Deep. Hard. Until she began quivering under him. Until he was trembling as her sweet heat went into convulsions, pulling his balls tight up against him. Until their moans mirrored each other, and he found a rhythm that would get them there. Only then did he rise on his arms and stare into her eyes, watching them widen. And when she lifted her hips higher yet, and he pumped up inside her, her eyes shut. Her chin rose, legs pointed straight out, and she went wild beneath him. His climax hit with little warning, burning up his spine until the pressure gave way to a fierce explosion that had him roaring with the intensity and pounding into her until he dropped down atop her, breathless and satisfied as her inner walls milked every drop he had to offer her.

He forced his mind back into his body. Amelia apparently had plans today, but so did he. He slowly withdrew his cock, inch by inch, feeling his seed escape down her thigh with him. Putting his weight on his arm, he shifted next to her, stroking her belly, waiting for her to acknowledge him. When she began to give a satisfied smile, he took that as the perfect opportunity for what he planned for next. Not hesitating, he reached behind the picture frame where he'd left a gift that his mother had given him in her will. He placed that gift on Amelia's belly.

Her eyes snapped opened and she gasped.

"This was my mother's engagement ring," he explained, softly. "My parents' story did not have a happy ending, but we will change that. We can make right what went so wrong in the Stone family." When she stared at him with huge eyes, but stayed silent, he continued, "I've been thinking about this for a long time. I know I pushed you away this past week. But I don't want to do that ever again. I want you to know every part of me. And I want to know every part of you. I know that you might not be ready for this, and we can take all the time you need. But this is what I want, Amelia. You, as my wife. It's what I've always wanted. To share in the pain. To share in the happiness. To rebuild my family. With you."

Her breath hitched. "I am ready for this. I'm ready for us, Beckett."

His heart squeezed and so many deep cracks began to seal as he took the ring from her belly and dangled it on his finger. "Amelia Carter, will you marry me?"

"Yes," she exclaimed. "Yes, of course, I'll marry you."

He slipped the ring onto her finger, and right as he slanted his mouth across hers, he heard a truck driving up his driveway. He'd recognize that rumble of an exhaust anywhere. "That's Nash, I'm sure of it."

"Oh, shit, we need to get dressed," Amelia gasped, jumping out of bed. "Hurry. Hurry."

"What is it?" he asked, not moving an inch.

She grabbed his arm, pulling him out of the bed. "You'll see. Get dressed."

Amelia re-dressed in record speed. Beckett was slower, and he left his shirt unbuttoned as he followed Amelia toward the front door. When she whisked the door opened, he froze, sure his eyes were wrong.

Nash stood by his truck, a big smile on his face. Behind that truck was a horse trailer and written on the side of that trailer read: BECKETT STONE. RIVER ROCK, COLORADO. He blinked and slowly looked at Amelia. "What is this?"

Her smile blinded him. "Your dream coming true."

## 15

Amelia kept hold of Beckett's hand, all but dragging him out of the house. It became pretty clear that since she'd last seen Beckett, he'd obviously had a change of heart about not sharing his pain with others, since he had his mother's ring ready to give to her. She loved knowing that one day she'd take his name and they'd have a family, but today she was going to change his life forever in the best way possible. That she was going to do what her sisters did for her. What Pops did for her.

Beckett stared at the horse trailer with his name written on the side before glancing sidelong at her. "I don't understand what's happening here."

"Well, you see," she said, hugging his arm, bouncing on her toes. "There was still that issue with the check I didn't want to take from you. The money that I know will always remain an issue between us that neither of us wants the other to take responsibility for. So, I did one better. I used the money for a good cause."

"I noticed you cashed the check," he said, his brows

furrowed tight. "And was glad for it, but…" He rubbed his chin, staring at the decal on the side of the gooseneck trailer before he focused on her again. "What is happening right now?"

She laughed at the blatant confusion swirling in his eyes. "I used the money to buy this horse trailer," she told him, and waited for his response.

He looked at Nash, as if he had the answers Beckett was looking to find, staring on in bewilderment. When Nash just grinned, Beckett asked her, "Why would you buy me a horse trailer?"

She twined her fingers in his, squinting at the sun in her eyes. "Over the past few days, I realized that I had Pops and my sisters always pushing me to do more, to chase my dreams, to never stop believing in myself. So that everyday I'm living my best life."

Beckett tilted his head, pursing his lips as he brushed his knuckles across her cheek. "I'm glad you had people to influence you, but I have no idea what that has to do with a horse trailer."

"This might clear this up a bit," Nash said. He moved to the trailer's side door and opened it. Autumn stuck her head out, and Larry had his head low enough to be seen too. "I figured that Autumn needed a buddy if she's going to live with you, and Amelia said she fell in love with Larry. We don't mind lending him out until you get some more horses on the property and find Amelia a good horse to join you on your rides."

Beckett's mouth parted, but he got interrupted as a couple of Nash's cowboys drove up. One truck had hay bales in the back. Another had grain, tack and farm supplies. As the trucks headed for the barn, Nash continued, "I've brought enough over to give you time to get these two settled and get yourself up and running." He gestured at Amelia. "Smart lady you've got here, setting all this up for you."

Amelia smiled, glad for Nash. When he heard her plan, he'd jumped on board fully, doing more than she even expected. Nash had all the contacts, so he made buying the trailer easy. She glanced to Beckett again, finding him scratching his cheek, so she set to explaining. "The plan is this: you're going to train with Autumn, and then when you're both ready, you're going to return to the rodeo. Nash said she's fast and can totally do this with you. This trailer will get you there and back to me."

Beckett blinked. "I'm going to return to the rodeo?"

"Yup," she said, so sure in this next step. "And if you're not going to do it for yourself, then you're going to do it for me. Because this is your dream. This was always your dream, and you deserve to at least have a shot at achieving it."

He slowly shook his head, though his eyes danced with a renewed light. "This is crazy. I've been out of the rodeo for so long. I'm too old for this. I haven't been training that hard, just throwing rope around for fun."

"So, what?" she countered. "You get back in it. You train hard again. You can most certainly do this. You can give yourself the right to go back to something you love and try again."

Beckett glanced out as a couple of the cowboys took Autumn and Larry off the trailer and headed toward the paddock with the shelter. All of which was still in perfect condition, which told Amelia she was right about this. He'd been in limbo, always waiting but never acting to fulfill his dream again, but this was Beckett's chance. When he looked her way again, he arched an eyebrow. "How will I pay my bills? You don't get paid for training. I won't make any money until I start winning."

"You'll be sponsored."

Beckett jerked his head back to Nash, who grinned at him and said, "Blackshaw Cattle and Blackshaw Horse Training are sponsoring you for the next two years. You'll wear our brands."

Amelia felt the tears threaten to rise but stuffed them away, as this was even news to her. Nash was a retired professional bull rider with a big name in the rodeo. Wearing his brand would bring other sponsorships.

"Nash," Beckett said, slowly. "I can't—"

"It's already done," Nash said, not leaving any room to argue. He left his spot by the trailer to settle at the bottom of the porch steps. "I'd like you to continue working for me, if you're interested. I'll send you some horses that can live here, and we'll keep the same arrangement when the horse sells. But when you're competing, we'll simply take the sales horses out of the equation, and you can focus on training."

Beckett looked on as the cowboys began taking the hay bales into the barn. "This is insane," he told them.

"It's not insane," Amelia snapped, shaking his arm. "It's right. It's time to go back to what you were meant to do. You deserve this, Beckett. You deserve to fight for this dream and make it happen."

Beckett blew out a long breath, staring out at his land then wrapped an arm around her neck. "You did this? All for me?"

"Yes, because I love you and I want you to be happy."

"Christ, Amelia, do I love you." Suddenly, she was gathered in his arms. He hugged her so tight she could barely breath, but she didn't want it any other way. "I can't believe you did this all for me. What if I don't succeed? It's a lot to risk."

"You will succeed," she said, without a single doubt in her mind.

Beckett just shook his head like he was having a hard time

processing all this. Tight in his arms, he asked Nash, "You sure about this?"

Nash nodded, stepping up to the last porch step and grinned. "Not a doubt in my mind. Just do me proud when you're out there kicking ass." He gestured back at Autumn. "She's fast and has talent and trusts you. Trust her back. With her breeding, she'll get you in the top rankings."

Beckett released Amelia and took Nash in a rough hug. "Not sure I can ever thank you for this, Nash."

"You don't need to ever thank me," Nash said. He turned away then glanced back with a tender smile, gesturing to Amelia's ring. "But I'll take an invite to your wedding." Apparently, Beckett had told Nash he planned to propose, and Amelia's heart nearly exploded in happiness out of her chest.

"That's a given," Amelia said with a big smile, and stepped back into Beckett's open arms, so glad Beckett had Nash on his side and in his life. "Thank you so much for everything, Nash."

He nodded gently, then approached the field with Autumn and Larry.

Amelia laughed as Larry ate the hay, looking bored, while Autumn ran around the field checking out her new home.

Beckett suddenly spun her into him. He stared down at her, a warm smile on his face, his arms tight around her. "For the record, I still think this is madness. Who knows if I can shoot up the ranks again? It's been years since I've timed myself to see if I'm even capable of competing at that level."

"Well, then, time yourself, and if your time sucks, train harder," she said, angling her head back and smiling up at him. "That's all there is to it."

Beckett drew in long, deep breath, glancing out as Nash approached Autumn and Larry in the field. "Why do I have a feeling that life is about to get a whole lot different?" he asked, returning his gaze to hers.

"Because it is," she said, grinning. "This is our time, Beckett."

He dropped his mouth on her lips and said against them, "Best damn thing I've heard in long time."

A year had gone by in a whirlwind of happy changes, and Amelia felt the greatest of those changes kicking her tummy as she served the older gentleman at her booth in the National Western Coliseum a can of Rugged Cowboy, the name they decided to call Beckett's beer that she created. Right as she moved to serve another customer, someone called her name. She looked around the stadium and found Hayes waving at her.

"It's time," Hayes yelled from the stands. "Amelia, it's time."

She quickly glanced at Penelope. "Do you mind holding down the fort?"

"Oh yeah," Penelope said. "We got this."

Amelia smiled, looking past Penelope, finding Clara and Maisie busy serving up beers to customers and her breath caught in her throat. Tonight was the last night they'd do an event together, and they all felt the weight of that. But the brewery had grown so much in the last year, after Ronnie liked not only a few samples of her beer, but all six, and marketed the hell out of them. Amelia had been able to hire staff to brew beer at the brewery. Clara now had an assistant. And while Penelope still handled the beer tours and special events, she had staff beneath her too—staff that would run these events without the sisters. Because life had changed dramatically for all of them. Maisie and Hayes were married at their house in a small ceremony a month after Beckett proposed. Beckett and Amelia's wedding followed a month later at his home, so that a part of his family touched their day. In the months that followed, Clara had a baby girl, Raelynn, and Maisie had a boy they named Cody. And now Amelia was five months pregnant, and everyone wanted to be home with their families, not out late at stadiums. Beckett had sold his father's property and had invested some of his inheritance into the brewery. So, when Amelia moved out of Pops' house and into Beckett's farm, they had used the money and converted the upstairs of Pops house into offices, and the lower floor had been renovated and turned into a taproom, serving burgers and homemade kettle chips, among other appetizers. Only the taproom had taken off too, and they were busier than ever. The brewery hadn't only become successful, it outshined the dream any of them had for it, and happiness and love settled over her family. That would have made Pops proud.

Clara took one look at Amelia and waved her off. "Go. We're fine here."

"Good luck," Maisie said, before turning back to her customer.

Amelia left the booth and hurried to Hayes' side before following him down the stairs to the seats the stadium gave them. She grabbed onto the railing, her heart leaping into her throat as she spotted Beckett in the gate behind the barrier.

Only one second later, the calf ran from the gate and Autumn took off, and Amelia screamed in encouragement as Beckett took one swing and let the rope fly. Amelia grabbed

Hayes' arm, holding tight the moment Beckett hit the ground running. Now trained and proving herself every step of the way, Autumn backed up, pulling the rope tight as Beckett grabbed the calf's flank and the rope, then had the calf on the ground. In mere seconds, he tied the calf's front end and the two back legs together before throwing his hands up. The crowd went wild, and Amelia death gripped Hayes' arms. "Did he do it?" she yelled over the crowd. "Did he do it?"

"Six, thirty-eight," Hayes said. "He had to have done it."

A moment later, the announcer said over the loudspeakers, "I would say he earned this championship." The crowd continued to roar as the announcer added, "Yup, he's done it. Ladies and gentlemen, give a round of applause to Beckett Stone, 2021 tie-down roping World Champion."

The crowd went wild in the stadium, and Amelia grabbed Hayes and hugged him tight, albeit awkwardly with her round belly. "He did it. He did it!"

Hayes hugged her back tight and laughed. "Hell, yeah, he did."

Beckett's smile nearly caused Amelia's heart to burst out of her chest. She remembered that smile. She saw it the day she married him. But this, this was all for him. This was his dream coming true.

Tears flooded her face as he scanned the crowd, and then his gaze met hers. He turned Autumn a little and then trotted over. Amelia leaned down over the railing as best she could with her pregnant belly in the way, the roaring of the crowd feeling like a giant hug around her, as he told her, "You did this. This is all you."

She laughed and cupped his face. "*You* did this. This was all you. It's always been right where you should be. I'm so proud of you, Beckett."

His smile was sweet and all the things she hoped for him. "I love you, Am."

"Love you back, cowboy." Not caring that a whole stadium of people were watching, she kissed him. In the same way she'd kissed him from the first time her lips met his. Exactly the way she kissed him when she married him. How she'd kiss him for the rest of her life. She kissed him like she belonged only to him, always to him, and he belonged to her.

# ABOUT THE AUTHOR

Stacey Kennedy is a *USA Today* bestselling author who writes contemporary romances full of heat, heart, and happily ever afters. With over 50 titles published, her books have hit Amazon, B&N, and Apple Books bestseller lists.

Stacey lives with her husband and two children in southwestern Ontario—in a city that's just as charming as any of the small towns she creates. Most days, you'll find her enjoying the outdoors with her family or venturing into the forest with her horse, Priya. Stacey's just as happy curled up indoors, where she writes surrounded by her lazy dogs. She believes that sexy books about hot cowboys or alpha heroes can fix any bad day. But wine and chocolate help too.

## ACKNOWLEDGMENTS

To my husband, my children, family, friends, and bestie, it's easy to write about love when there is so much love around me. Big thanks to my readers for all their support of the Carter sisters and the River Rock world; my editor, Lexi Smail, for being her amazing self who sprinkles her magic all over my books; my agent, Jessica Alvarez, for her endless support; my cover artist, Regina Wamba, who blew me away with the covers for this series with her beautiful work; to Rose Perry for stepping in when I needed her most; my PR company, Social Butterfly PR, I'd be lost without you; Shayla Black, Angel Payne, my sprinting buddies, who keep me focused and make my writing days fun; Kennedy Layne, the best writing buddy a girl could ask for. Thank you.

Want to spend more time in River Rock? Check out Penelope's story in:

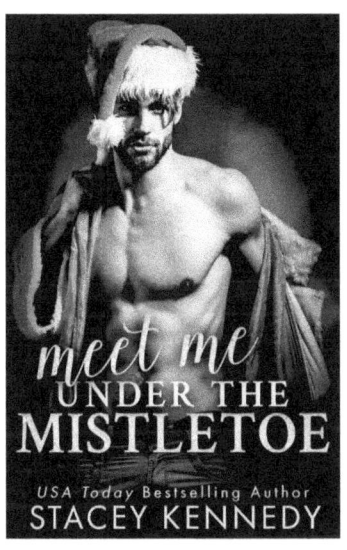

# CHAPTER 1

*"He knows if you've been bad or good..."* the long-haired brunette with the sparkling green eyes sang.

These days, not much gathered a crowd large enough to warrant a call to 911, but tonight was definitely not an ordinary night. The wrought-iron streetlights beamed soft light down on the sidewalk along River Rock's historic Main Street, revealing large snowflakes fluttering down as Officer Darryl Wilson strode up to the large fountain in the center of town. The small town nestled into the Colorado mountains saw less crime than Disneyland on any given day. There hadn't been a murder in River Rock since sometime in the 1970s, and most crime was either teenagers stirring up trouble, shady businessmen, domestic disputes, or more likely, drunk tourists getting into shenanigans. This time, just before eleven o'clock at night, the trouble was an intoxicated woman skating on the fountain in her high heels. And as he stepped closer, Darryl couldn't believe his eyes.

Penelope Carter. He'd heard she'd come back to town a few days ago, but he wasn't expecting to see her like this.

The girl who'd blown his mind at summer camp with the

hottest kiss of his life when he was a camp counselor and then abruptly bailed, leaving him to never hear from her again, was skating before him. She'd been a pretty girl back then. She'd grown into a gorgeous woman with curves in all the right places that had his full attention.

"Santa Claus is coming to town," Penelope continued singing, pushing off one heel and lifting her hands in the air as if she were a figure skater and the music was real, not in her head.

Impressive, really. She skated better on heels than most people did on skates.

Darryl sighed and took in the crowd next to her with their cell phones out filming Penelope. She was going to regret this in the morning, especially if her little skit went viral. "All right," he said, stepping forward. "Tuck those phones away. The show is over."

A few grumbles later, the glow of the cell phones faded, and the crowd began to dissipate. Darryl turned back to Penelope, who sang, "You better watch out." At least if the clip went viral, she could carry a note.

"Penelope," he said, closing in on her, experiencing the same building heat he'd felt with her all those years ago.

She did a little twirl. "You better not pout." She pushed off one heel, wobbling slightly then quickly righted herself. "Something, something, something...gonna find out who's naughty or nice."

He chuckled. Christ, ten years ago, Penelope had been a mix of sexy and cute. That hadn't changed since he'd last seen her. He moved closer, not wanting the paperwork that came with an injury. Just like all those years ago, he couldn't take his eyes off her. He'd been as enthralled with her when she was a teenager. The night he'd given her that *hot* kiss, she'd worn tiny shorts and her exposed belly had been his entire focus. Even now, in her tight sweater and black leggings, she stirred things inside him that hadn't been stirred in a while.

The trouble with small towns, and being a cop, was Darryl knew *everyone,* and they knew that he and his ex-wife, Natalie, had divorced six months ago. Natalie had left town before the ink of the divorce papers had dried, and every well-meaning woman in town had been trying to help him "get over" his grief.

Now, Penelope had turned up, and he wondered if fate were giving him a chance to revisit his past. Unfortunately, it appeared that Penelope was in the habit of skirting the law. A law that Darryl had spent the past eight years enforcing. He'd put in his due and worked the night shifts since River Rock PD hired him. With a few cops retiring the next few months, there would be upcoming promotions, and the captain had already given Darryl the heads-up to bring his A game for the next while.

A promotion that he already fumbled once six months ago when Larry Michaels retired. The day Natalie had signed the divorce papers and left him, Darryl decided to spend the evening making friends with a bottle of whisky. He'd also made a complete ass out of himself at the local watering hole in town, Kinky Spurs. The next day, the promotion went to another cop.

That couldn't happen again.

Penelope sang another few lines, turning in a tight circle, and Darryl honestly doubted he could handle the likes of a grown-up Penelope Carter.

"Santa Claus—" Penelope screamed, as her heel caught on the edge of the fountain.

Darryl lurched forward when she began to fall. She landed with a yelp in his arms, and her wide green eyes connected with his. "All right?" he asked, ignoring the way her long, chocolate-colored hair felt damn soft against his hand.

Their gazes held for a beat. Then, she burst out laughing. A full-on belly laugh. One that Darryl never thought he'd ever experienced in his life.

"It's you," she finally said when she stopped laughing.

"It's me," he replied, ignoring the semi he was sporting from holding her so close. She smelled like sugar and vanilla, pure temptation.

"It's you," she repeated, snuggling her face into him like she belonged there. "Has anyone ever told you that you're warm and comfy, just like a big teddy bear?"

"I'm warm because it's freezing outside, and you're wearing only a sweater." He slowly placed her down, ensuring she was steady. When he let her go, he unzipped his coat and slid it over her shoulders. "And you are very drunk."

She giggled, her eyes bright. "I know. I think it was the forth." She held up her finger and hiccupped. "Nope, the fifth shot that did me in." She pulled his jacket around her, inhaling a big deep breath then grinning at him. "Seriously, you still smell so damn yummy. How is that even possible?"

Yeah, and he was rock hard now. Focusing away from what his little brain wanted, he turned to the laughing crowd who had obviously returned when Penelope fell. "I said the show was over, folks," he told them firmly. "Go home before anyone else gets in trouble."

"Oh, is that what I am...*in trouble*?"

Darryl's jaw clenched at the heat and promise in her voice before turning back to her. He found her heady gaze on him, lust burning through him. Or maybe it wasn't lust but the alcohol making her eyes glossy. "Come on, you little trouble-maker. It's bedtime for you."

"Your bed, I hope." She grinned, pressing all those hot curves against him.

"Not tonight." *But maybe some night.* He shook the thought from his head, knowing this woman was not the type of woman for him to play around with. She'd likely be more of a headache than what it was worth. With his possible upcoming promotion, he could not have a smudge on his image, and this stunt was enough to tell him that he needed to stay clear of her. He took her gently by the arm and led her to the car, opening the door for her.

"So, you really a cop?" she asked, flopping into the passenger seat. "Can I see your handcuffs?"

"Yes, I am." He leaned down. "And no, you may not."

"Boo. How boring." She laughed.

Hyper aware of her in every regard, he reached for the seat belt then clipped her in.

"See, Mr. Police Officer, you like getting all close to me," she purred.

He turned his head after hearing the click, his mouth resting close enough to hers that all he needed to do was lean a little forward to claim those pouty lips. One little inch for him to find out if she still tasted as sweet as she smelled. "I don't recall having said that I didn't," he told her honestly.

His answer obviously surprised her, as her eyes widened ever so slightly. He grinned to himself, intrigued by the possibility he could surprise a woman like Penelope Carter. From what he learned from her cousins over the years, she'd been traveling and bartending her way along the coast. She'd seen it all, done it all, and experienced everything. But maybe one thing she hadn't seen was small-town life and a man like Darryl, who had promised himself to no longer keep quiet about what he wanted and be as honest and straightforward as possible. He'd compromised enough with his ex-wife, Natalie.

At Penelope's silence, he arched an eyebrow. Yeah, he'd

play this game, and he'd play it better than her. "Nothing else to add, Ms. Carter?" he asked.

Her eyes rolled a little. "Ugh. I'm really drunk."

"I see that." He grabbed a plastic bag from this glove box and laid it out open on her lap. "If you're going to be sick, use the bag." He ensured her legs were all tucked in, his fingers tightening to linger there, and then he shut the door. He strode back to the driver's side door, a cloud of his breath leading the way, when suddenly the lights and siren flicked on, electrifying the dark night. "Trouble, yeah, sugar, that's you." He hurried into the car, flicking off the siren when he dropped into the seat, then he turned the ignition on and mumbled, "Can't seem to keep your hands to yourself, little menace. Police cars aren't toys." He turned to her. "Are you staying with your cousins?" His gaze hit those gorgeous legs again before moving up her body until he reached her face. She rested her head against the headrest, her face tilted toward him, her eyes shut. "Penelope." A beat. "Penelope."

She snored softly.

"It's not even a full moon," he grumbled and sighed. He reached over and gave her a little shake. "Penelope."

*Nothing.*

He stared at her then dropped his head back on his headrest, considering the best option now. He could call her cousins, the three Carter sisters who owned Three Chicks Brewery—a local craft brewery that was looking for its big break getting their locally famous beer, Foxy Diva distributed within North America—to find out where Penelope was staying. But somehow, that felt like the wrong move. The other choice was taking her to the station's drunk tank, but that wasn't quite right either.

"Let's just hope your trouble doesn't become *my* trouble," he told her before putting the car in drive.

www.ingramcontent.com/pod-product-compliance
Lightning Source LLC
Chambersburg PA
CBHW051957220626
47052CB00004B/978